Hauser's Memory

Forrest J Ackerman Presents
Hauser's Memory
by Curt Siodmak

PULPLESS.COM, INC.
775 East Blithedale Ave., Suite 508
Mill Valley, CA 94941, USA.
Voice & Fax: (500) 367-7353
Home Page: http://www.pulpless.com/
Business inquiries to info@pulpless.com
Editorial inquiries & submissions to
editors@pulpless.com

First Pulpless.Com™, Inc. Edition August, 1999.
Library of Congress Catalog Card Number: 99-62099
ISBN: 1-58445-117-3

Book and Cover designed by CaliPer, Inc.
Cover Illustration by Billy Tackett, Arcadia Studios
© 1999 by Billy Tackett

For the three A's, my Ph.D. friends:
Allan, who succeeded in transferring the memory of a
hamster to a rat;
Arnold, for whom no idea is too abstract to be tried out in a
laboratory;
Arthur, who had the patience to read through the
manuscript and gave advice and help.

And for the new generation: Carol and Lynn.

Table of Contents

CHAPTER   PAGE

Introduction by Forrest J Ackerman 9

1 11

2 23

3 29

4 37

5 45

6 51

7 55

8 61

9 65

10 73

11 77

12 85

13 97

14 105

15 117

16 123

17 131

18 139

19 155

20 169

21 179

22 183

23 199

24 215

25 225

26 231

Introduction by
Forrest J Ackerman

Remember Dr. Cory, the brilliant scientist of *Donovan's Brain?*

Well, he's back in the sequel to Siodmak's hallmark science fiction novel. The unique Siodmakian imagination that has captured millions of readers around the world for the past half century (in just about every language but Esperanto) continues to weave its spell herewith in *Hauser's Memory.*

These classics are back thanks to Pulpless.Com, Inc.!

1

The man handed Dr. Cory his card: "Francis L. Slaughter." No address. Nothing about his profession. Cory put the card down and waited. A couple of hours ago the dean of the university had asked him to talk to the man. A call had come from Washington introducing Slaughter. It had not revealed his mission.

Slaughter was tall and loose-limbed, with close-cropped red hair and a face with uneven halves, one side full, the other more alert and tense. His nose was long and thin, moving in small circles like an opossum's sniffing the air as if to detect the presence of danger. He was about forty years old, dressed in gray, sporting a gray tie.

"I work for a department of the government that dislikes publicity," Slaughter said. "Science research has become so important to national defense that the President has had to create a special department within another department to keep tabs on its progress. It is then applied to diplomacy, to the Pentagon, and others."

He emphasized the word "others" and looked at Cory covertly.

Cory said nothing.

"We're interested m your experiments with RNA," Slaughter continued, "very interested. Since you are the foremost expert in that field, Dr. Cory, I want you to know I believe the ribonucleic acids can change the pattern of our social structure."

"All things are possible," Cory muttered.

Slaughter still had not got the opening he was looking for. "DNA and RNA are part of the genetic mechanism that controls the hereditary trends in humans and animals. DNA is the genetic code, RNA is its prophet." Slaughter enjoyed the opportunity to demonstrate his newly acquired knowledge. He had read all the material he could find about this very recent field in biochemistry, though most of it, even articles in the popular magazines, was very complex. "We are aware that research is being conducted by biochemists and psychologists in many universities all over the world." He threw one long leg over the other and smiled, closing his mouth like a guillotine. "My mission is very confidential. Your latest experiments have made it possible. If it works out, we will have won a battle. We are at war, Dr. Cory, and wars are won with weapons. RNA could be one of them."

"Please come to the point," Cory said. Platitudes made him impatient. "You didn't come all the way from Washington to tell me about the importance of RNA."

But it was not easy to provoke Slaughter. He had been trained to divorce his missions from his emotions. "I believe we should have a preliminary talk before I tell you my department's request. I don't want to shock you."

"Don't be afraid of that."

"I base your probable reaction on mine," Slaughter went on. "When I was told the message I was to deliver to you, I couldn't believe it at first. For security reasons it couldn't very well be put in a letter, and we are pressed for time, so I was told to see you in person."

When Cory still looked at him without expression, Slaughter decided to approach from a different angle.

"I understand that you're a medical doctor as well as a biochemist."

"You ought to know my background as well as I do," Cory answered. "I once saw the file the FBI keeps on me. It looked like a volume of the *Encyclopaedia Britannica.* I'm sure the CIA has access to the FBI files."

Slaughter made no acknowledgment of Cory's reference to the Central Intelligence Agency, but his opossum nose again twitched. With a long arm he pulled an ashtray closer and snuffed out his cigarette.

"This room isn't bugged by any chance?" he asked with mock concern. "Top-secret conversations like these usually take place outside, on a walk, say, to make bugging impossible." Gliding his fingers under the table, he looked around the small office. It contained a desk, two steel chairs, file cabinets. It had neither curtains nor rug. The window overlooked a small square and the side of the chemistry building. Not an inspiring room, but then Slaughter didn't seem really concerned about being overheard.

"No microphones," said Cory, who, for all his experience with government supervision, had had no previous contacts with Washington departments. Slaughter was the first official to come see him.

"Five days ago," Slaughter said, suddenly rising to his feet, "a German scientist defected from the Russians. His coming over to our side is as important as, say, getting hold of the blueprints of the Russian antimissile missiles —which he helped construct, by the way. He showed up in West Berlin and asked for asylum. We wanted to fly him out to Washington, but at the Tempelhof airport he was shot; the bullet hit his spine and paralyzed him. Of course, the Russians didn't want him to deliver that file cabinet in his brain to us. The police arrested the assassin, but that didn't help him or us."

The regret in his voice was an accusation: it seemed to say, had he been in charge, the incident wouldn't have happened.

"Did he die?" Cory asked. He couldn't guess why Slaughter was telling him the story.

"No. He's still in a coma," Slaughter said in the same accusing voice. "We're keeping him alive with everything in the book. But we can't communicate with him. He might die any moment, taking with him the information we hoped to get."

"That still doesn't explain why you've come to the department of biochemistry."

Slaughter lowered his voice. "Dr. Cory, you have succeeded in transferring memory from one animal to another."

"So did Holger Hyden in Goteborg and McConnel at the University of Michigan and groups in other places."

"But you're the only one who has succeeded with highly developed animals, like dogs and monkeys. The next step would be with human beings, wouldn't it?"

Cory smiled thinly. "Are you suggesting we transfer your defector's memory to another human brain?"

Slaughter grinned. He had maneuvered Cory where he wanted him. He bent forward. "Could it be done? Or would such an attempt be just too fantastic?"

"Cameron has given human beings yeast RNA both intravenously and orally. He also succeeded in isolating human RNA, but human RNA injected into living tissues might create a violent reaction. It could be fatal."

"We may have to take that chance," Slaughter said, sitting down.

"We haven't advanced enough in our research to take such a drastic step," protested Cory. "RNA is quite toxic, and we haven't yet succeeded in eliminating or separating its toxic quality. I'd hate to be responsible for the death of a human being." He added sardonically, "It wouldn't show up favorably in my files."

"Don't worry about that," Slaughter said. "We would assume the responsibility." Ritually he lit another cigarette. "You have, of course, thought of working with humans."

"Ultimately."

"Where would you get volunteers for your experiments?"

"I have stacks of letters from people who want to submit themselves to the test."

"Why should they want to do that? Curiosity?"

"Partly. Some are terminal cases and want to do something

for humanity before the curtain falls. Others have patriotic reasons. Everyone has a reason, Mr. Slaughter. But as you know, our laws forbid this kind of experimenting on people. Even if they volunteer we are not permitted to accept them. It's different in other countries."

"But aren't you corresponding with Canada and Sweden about just that—using their volunteers?"

"I see you open letters," Cory said coldly. "Do you also tap telephones?"

"Of course. You might have observed that we haven't bothered you," Slaughter answered, as if this made amends for his activities.

"And just how do you propose going about it? RNA has to be extracted from tissues, you know. There are RNA molecules in every body cell, but we'd have to use those exclusively in the brain. Your man from the East is still alive. That's a slight obstacle, isn't it? Or do you intend to accelerate his death?"

"Indeed not!" Slaughter seemed genuinely shocked. "But you can start as soon as the man is pronounced dead." Slaughter apparently was fully convinced of Cory's cooperation. "I believe that some tissues stay alive until *rigor mortis* sets in."

"Possibly," Cory answered "But can you arrange his death for the moment that's most convenient for the test?"

Slaughter disregarded the insinuation. "According to medical reports, our man has no chance of surviving the night. When has a man died? That's a medical question not even a doctor can always answer. For me, he's already dead."

"Where is he? Still in Berlin?"

"At the moment he's here—at the General Hospital."

Cory stared at him in amazement.

"We contemplate moving him closer to your equipment. Would you recommend that we take him to the Medical Center here at the campus?"

He seems to take my cooperation for granted. Cory thought.

"Of course, the decision is up to you," Slaughter continued smoothly. "But since we have to act fast, I don't see any alternative. There is no one else of your ability and experience in Europe or here in America. You're the only one who can provide even a dim chance of success.

"No personal involvement of any kind for you in this case, of course. The donor of the RNA will remain anonymous. We won't tell you his name or burden you with unnecessary information. Secrets are most disturbing for people unused to them. I have found that the more intelligent a person is, the less he can keep a secret."

For Cory, experiments on animals were routine. The animal itself was a technical detail, like a Skinner box or electronic equipment. Animals had to be regarded without sentiment otherwise experiments would be impossible. But to use human RNA on a man who might die from the test!

"I'd need to make exhaustive tests," Cory said slowly, "before I could start such an experiment."

"We don't have time."

"The test would require a volunteer."

"We've taken care of that. We will deliver someone to you, willing, eager, and, of course, very healthy."

"Where did you find him? In your department?" Cory looked at Slaughter with an ironical smile. "Or are you going to try RNA out on yourself?"

"On me?" Slaughter laughed. "Not a chance! I'm nonexistent. A messenger. A mailman."

It seemed that he had hurdled all the obstacles. All that remained was to deliver the dying man's memory molecules and the human guinea pig to Cory.

"I can't give you an answer right now," Cory said.

Slaughter's face lengthened, implacable, relentless. "We regard you as a man working on his own problems, not exclusively for the university, so there's a substantial fee involved, of course. Very substantial." He put his hand in his breast pocket as if to withdraw a wad of money. "We would engage you in your private capacity, thus avoiding any possible embarrassment for the university."

"I wouldn't and I couldn't divorce myself from the university."

Slaughter was too smart to press for a decision, and got up. "I'm staying at the Beverly Hills Hotel, bungalow seven. Why don't you come over for a drink this afternoon?"

"I'll call you," Cory said "I must also talk this over with my assistant."

"I thought you were the boss," Slaughter said.

"In my field no one is 'boss.' I depend on many brains to solve the riddles confronting me. Even so-called experts know very little about RNA in memory."

As soon as Slaughter had left, Cory tried to call Hillel Mondoro at the chemistry department. For the last three years Hillel had been Cory's chemist for all his experiments The telephone in his office rang, but no one answered. Cory guessed he might be downstairs in one of the laboratories. New equipment had arrived, and Hillel would be there to watch the electricians installing it. A stickler for perfection, Hillel liked to be informed of everything new in the department of chemistry and biochemistry.

The building was strangely quiet, although it was a working day. Usually a mixture of sounds floated through the corridors: the hum of oscillators and motors, telephones ringing. He entered the small library on the second floor, deserted except for two girls looking for a book on molecular biology.

"Have you seen the Hershey and Case, Dr. Cory?" one of them asked, impatiently tossing back a shock of auburn hair.

"It's not supposed to be taken from the library," Cory said.

"Then somebody must've swiped it," the second girl said disgustedly.

"I have a copy," Cory said to the redhead. "You can have it for a week. I'll be back in my office in half an hour."

"Thanks, Dr. Cory." She smiled at him.

"Where's Goldberg?" Cory asked. Goldberg, the nickname the students gave Hillel Mondoro, is Mondoro translated into German. Sometimes he was called Mont d'Or, pronounced with an exaggerated French accent. He was well liked, or the students wouldn't have bothered to make good-natured fun of him.

"It's Yom Kippur," the red-haired girl said. "The Jews aren't here today; that's why it's so quiet." There was no innuendo implied; she would have said "French" or "Spanish" the same way.

"Mont d'Or told us that he wouldn't be in today," her friend said. "As if we didn't know! My boyfriend didn't show up either. Funny, he's not religious Except on Yom Kippur."

"Atavistic drive," the redhead said. "I wonder if it's the RNA or the DNA molecules in him. What do you think, Dr. Cory?"

Cory had not realized it was a Jewish holiday No wonder the department was almost deserted. The percentage of Jews in theoretical physics and biochemistry was high in comparison to their number on campus. Perhaps their intellectual grounding in the Talmud had trained them to think in abstractions. Maybe Lysenko's idea might find a basis one of these days, Cory thought. Who can say which law is right and which wrong? Laws are manmade; science moves in phases. Knowledge, Cory had found out, was never definite, only tentative.

He walked down the stairs to where the laboratory animals were kept. Like jail, the doors could be opened only with a passkey.

Minnie, the chimpanzee, greeted him with a squeal of joy and pressed a button, which should have produced a banana for her. Cory put one in a container attached to the cage.

"Try now," Cory told her. Again she pressed the red button,

and the banana slid into her cage. Peeling it daintily, Minnie threw back her head and grinned—amazingly like the redhead upstairs!

She had not been caught to press buttons for reward; she had inherited the skill from her former mate, Oscar. Oscar had been sacrificed, his RNA injected into her. Minnie had remembered Oscar's tricks. She had also developed idiosyncrasies that Cory had observed in Oscar: his dislike of certain students, his rejection of certain foods which Minnie had enjoyed before the RNA injection. Were Minnie's new habits the result of Oscar's transferred RNA? How long would it have taken for Minnie to learn Oscar's tricks without his RNA molecules in her system? Those questions had to be solved before a human experiment could be attempted.

Slaughter's demand was dangerous.

Cory picked up the telephone and dialed Hillel's home Hillel's wife, Karen, answered.

"He's in *shul*," she said, "but he'll be back in the afternoon. Yom Kippur's over by dark."

"Late in the afternoon," Cory repeated, realizing that it would be too late to discuss Slaughter's experiment with Hillel.

"Come over and have dinner with us." Karen sounded gay, as always. "When the sun is down we can *anbeissen.* And I did my best to cook well for tonight. That's not difficult. Hillel's mother is a lousy cook, but he thinks she's tops. It's just a matter of not letting the food burn, as she does. No 'mother's spice'!"

"Anbeissen." The word was new to Cory. He liked Karen, her cockiness, which Hillel called *chuzpah,* her grace and youth.

"Having the first bite after the fast," Karen explained. "I'll have to teach you Yiddish and make you part of our inner circle." She laughed.

She was a slender, dark-haired girl with the face of Nefertiti and the graceful movements of the Sephardic Jews. Cory liked the way she walked, very straight, her crown of jet-black hair shimmering as if it were lacquer. She wore no makeup except for a line framing her eyelids and red lipstick boldly accentuating her generous mouth. Hillel had met her at the university, where she was studying dramatics. She seemed born to be married to him.

"Is there a way of getting in touch with him?" Cory asked.

"You can't go to *shul.* They won't let you in without a ticket. Don't you know that the Jews can't pray on holidays if they haven't paid admission to the synagogue? Before the ceremony starts, they throw out all the deadbeats who sneak into the temple to pray for free. Disgusting, those crooks!"

She laughed with slight embarrassment. Karen did not share Hillel's Orthodoxy, though she had adjusted herself to his way of life.

"Don't tell Hillel that I was looking for him," Cory said. "I don't want to disturb his holiday."

"Of course I won't. You can tell him yourself tonight. We expect you for dinner. Good-bye. I smell something burning!"

The receiver clicked. Cory suspected this was a ruse to prevent any objection on his part.

He had never, even as a child, taken part in other people's activities. Always he was driven by *Torschlusspanik,* the fear that he might run out of time and not be able to accomplish enough in his lifetime. He allotted himself four hours' sleep, got up at four in the morning to read the latest scientific publications until seven, then walked to the campus, using this time to think out problems His father was an Irish immigrant who wanted to see his only child a scholar. He had forced the boy to study. Cory had completed high school at fourteen and was the youngest student ever to receive a Ph.D. in biochemistry from the University of Chicago. But too much studying had dried up Cory's emotions, as he discovered when he married. His wife, who had more intelligence than looks, complained that his secretary saw him more than she did. At thirty-eight he received the Nobel Prize for having discovered the molecular construction of ribonucleic acids and their function in storing in the memories of warm-blooded animals. When his wife suddenly died, Cory withdrew still more. He was offered professorships at several universities and chose California, not because of its climate but because of a discussion with the university's president.

"We will never inquire about your choice of projects," the president said. "You are completely free to do whatever you want to do, and you'll have our full cooperation."

Cory had come a long way from the first experiments with marine flatworms, cannibal platyhelminths. He had trained thousands of them to follow a light to find food. Their RNA injected into untrained flatworms, one worm getting the concentrated RNA of hundreds of its predecessors, turned the untrained worms at once toward the light in search of food. He had conditioned hamsters to press a bar to get a pellet of food. Their RNA injected into untrained rats also produced memory transfer. The rats went straight to the bars, pressed them, and picked up the morsels that fell into the bowls.

Cory liked to teach addressing himself to a choice selection of students. Science was in flux, and an answer to a problem might come from any one of them. The discovery that memory is influenced and perhaps directed by certain chemicals had opened a new world of research. The theoretical variations were limitless: if one species could be injected with a serum containing the memory traits of another species, a monkey could be changed into a smart human being, a dog might be made to act like a cat. One could preserve the knowledge of highly trained older people by transferring it to younger brains. The more biochemistry found out that the human body reacted to chemicals that thought and emotion could be induced by chemicals, that man was purely a chemical factory, the more the age-old concepts of man's soul and divine ordination had to be reexamined.

Cory could talk about these ideas with Hillel; they were the only interests in his life. For Hillel, Cory was a prophet, and he looked up to him like a disciple, convinced that Cory's superior mind would be able to solve not only scientific but also the social problems brought by the very speed of scientific discovery.

Cory went back to his office. The student with the auburn hair was waiting, and he gave her the book she wanted.

Then he picked up the telephone and called the Beverly Hills Hotel. He had to give Slaughter an answer.

2

Francis Lovejoy Slaughter picked up a couple of messages at the desk of his hotel. One was from Washington, the other from the General Hospital. He walked across the garden to bungalow seven. Once inside, he locked the door and sniffed the air to make sure he had had no visitors. Then he looked at the messages. "Call anytime"— that was from Dr. Nettor at the General Hospital. It meant that Hauser was still alive and there was no likelihood that he would die in the next few hours and take his secrets with him. The other call had to be answered at once. He picked up the telephone and gave the operator an unlisted number in Washington, D.C.

"Twelve-two," Slaughter said into the receiver. A moment later Colonel Borg, his immediate superior, was on the line.

"Francis," Borg said, low-voiced. He used Slaughter's first name whenever he was nervous or anxious. "I had a call from the penthouse. They want to be reassured."

The topmost offices were occupied by Borg's superiors. Borg treated Slaughter as an ally against the machinations from above. But there was no friendship between them. Slaughter considered all men his enemies.

The call from the penthouse was from Dr. Wendtland, the head of the Eastern European Affairs Department. Wendtland was a naturalized American who had worked himself into a sensitive position in the CIA. Before joining, he had ferreted out former Nazis in high positions in the German government. Slaughter suspected that he had been in touch with Hauser for a long time, maybe for years.

"Cory's playing coy," Slaughter said. "But he'll come around." He made no gratuitous comments. He knew Borg was taping the conversation.

"Do you really expect this crazy thing will come off?"

"We shot an arrow in the air...." Slaughter laughed. "If I'd been asked a year ago to go through with such an operation, I'd have thought it crazy. But now I don't dare doubt anything those boys cook up in their labs."

"How's California?" Borg asked.

Slaughter looked around the bungalow. The sun filtered into the room. The door to the bedroom was open, revealing a king-sized bed, the mattress thick, the baroque headboard heavily carved. Famous movie stars had slept in that bed. How differently he lived: to be shadowy and anonymous was part of his profession.

"Hot. Dull. Lonely."

Borg laughed. "It wouldn't be for me. Well, make sure you go ahead and do whatever's necessary to make Cory happy. He's a bachelor, isn't he? The bungalow of an expensive hotel is the right place to entertain."

"That's the idea."

"I wish I were out there with you and could scout around for both of us. Of course, I expect a full report."

"Affirmative."

"And call me as soon as you know Cory's decision."

"Understood."

Slaughter hung up, feeling angry and discomforted. Why had Borg insinuated that he was promoting girls? Borg wants to get something on me, he concluded.

Like a transparent glass turning frosted, Slaughter reverted to his customary caution. He had little use for speculation; he had always dealt with concrete facts which could be set down in sensible reports. But the Hauser case had moved beyond reality. How could he have believed that transferring one man's memory to another man was really feasible? To the trained investigator, the whole idea was without substance.

But still, there was Cory's successful experiment with chimpanzees. Though Cory had not published his findings, Slaughter knew that he had transferred the memory of a trained chimpanzee to an untrained animal.

Biochemistry was only one step away from witchcraft, in Slaughter's opinion. Actually, Cory was lucky he lived in the twentieth century; in any other age he would have been burned at the stake. Slaughter had read all the material he could get on the subject. He had learned that DNA, the deoxyribonucleic acid in living matter (even the name smacked of abracadabra), contains the hereditary code of the species and determines why a mouse looks like a mouse and not like a flower or a bird; why some people are born with red hair and others with dark or blond; why some have a talent for music or mathematics; why a bird is able to build a nest without being taught—the instinctive memory; and why every species sings its distinctive song.

Cory had experimented with RNA, the ribonucleic acids. They are not the primary genetic code, that is DNA; they are translations of the DNA messages, like a wax impression of a key. However, some of the ribonucleic acids are different. These carry not the static memory of the species but the dynamic memory of the individual. Man and other animals learn by experience, which is repetition, shock, and imitation. Behavior is based on DNA-coded capacity acting with the RNA-coded memory carried in brain cells.

Although he did not understand clearly what he had read, Slaughter was fascinated by it all. But why had Borg chosen him, a layman, to observe Cory, and why had he assigned him to this intricate task?

Slaughter was a lawyer, with no background in science. Excessive knowledge beclouds the judgment, Borg told him; unlike laymen like Slaughter. experts are boxed in by theories. Borg wanted a man without scientific knowledge, and Slaughter was the man.

Walking about in the small bungalow three thousand miles

from Washington, Slaughter felt lost. He dialed the hospital's number. Dr. Nettor's voice sounded tired.

"How is he?" Slaughter asked.

"Fading. I've cleaned out the blood for the fourth time. Uremic poisoning. I don't give him more than a night."

"If you stop the kidney machine he dies?"

"Within an hour."

"Would he ever regain consciousness?"

"Not a chance. He has a massive subdural hematoma. He couldn't talk even if he were conscious. Nor could he move."

Slaughter's game of solitaire was coming to an end.

"Call Dr. Queen at the Medical Center at the campus. Tell him Cory needs a room for a terminal case."

"Is Cory going ahead with it?" Nettor asked.

"Of course. He's anxious to take over."

Nettor hung up.

Taking off his shoes, Slaughter stretched out on the movie stars' bed. But he couldn't relax. He jumped up and opened a window, and the subtropical heat hit him bodily. He closed the window quickly. His mouth felt dry and shriveled, and he poured himself a glass of ice water. It didn't help much.

Before he had moved to Washington, Slaughter was a junior partner in the New York law firm of Dutten, Hill, and Hill. He did some work for the FBI. A CIA official came across his lucid reports and offered him a position. Secrecy was an obsession with Slaughter, and he accepted immediately. He moved his family to Washington and traveled every day to the CIA headquarters in Langley. There, in the huge building, big even by Washington standards—it covered nine acres, contained a million square feet and was seven stories high—he occupied a room on the third floor. Now only a few people blocked his way to the top; one was Borg, another Wendtland.

It had been Slaughter's suggestion to fly Hauser by special plane from Berlin to Los Angeles. It was Slaughter's idea to approach Cory. He also procured a volunteer to receive the dying man's memory. He knew the top echelon in the penthouse was impressed by his daring and by the speed and precision with which he was handling this seemingly weird and hopeless case. Slaughter had shown imagination, a dangerous though highly appreciated quality.

Slaughter felt his breathing become shallow when he remembered the scene that brought Cory into the play. His nerves were taut. He needed a drink badly.

He never drank before six in the afternoon, a private rule that he had never broken. Washington, which consumes twice as much liquor as any other city in the country, had taught Slaughter the effects of uninhibited drinking. But there was that East/West time difference. Wasn't it after seven back East?

He put his hand on the telephone to call room service. Somebody else was on the line. Patrick Cory.

"I'd like to meet that volunteer of yours before I give you an answer," Cory said.

"Why?" Slaughter stalled. "I want to involve you as little as possible. Just regard the whole thing as another experiment."

"I'd like to ask him a few questions," Cory said, and Slaughter, his alarm increasing, knew he had to compromise.

"Why shouldn't you see him?" Slaughter put on another record, a cheerful one. "I'll have him here in half an hour. Will that be convenient for you?"

"I'll be there."

"We could have a couple of drinks and dinner."

"Sorry," Cory said. "It's Yom Kippur, and I'm invited to an *anbeissen.*"

"I didn't know you were Jewish." Slaughter sounded startled.

"Doesn't my file give my religion?"

"Your father was Irish and your mother French," Slaughter said. "Now you've conned me into admitting that I read your file." He laughed.

Cory hadn't expected him to have a sense of humor.

3

Slaughter watched the waiter set up the bar—a bottle of bourbon, one of gin, and one of Scotch. The waiter left, and at once he had the bourbon bottle in hand. "What's yours?" He held it with the reverence Cory associated with alcoholics.

"Scotch and water," Cory said, and Slaughter poured a generous serving.

"You have quite a heavy hand," he remarked, and Slaughter laughed.

"I could never get a job as a bartender," he said, and measured bourbon into a glass for himself. "Sorry you're invited elsewhere tonight. We could've had a nice time together."

He lifted the glass in a toast, took a sip, and rolled the liquid on his tongue.

"Yom Kippur," Slaughter said, as if weighing the words. "The man who invited you must be a very close friend. Jews rarely invite a Gentile on their highest holiday."

"I wouldn't describe it quite that way. It's just that Karen Mondoro is a good cook and I'm a bachelor."

Cory was watching Slaughter the way he observed a laboratory animal. That quick reassuring glance at the bottle, that jocular prying into Cory's life as though it were part of the conversation, that varnished insincerity hiding a ruthless character all made Cory wary.

"Mondoro." Slaughter repeated the name to make it sink into his memory. "Mondoro." He sat down, nursing his drink.

"My chemist. He's in on every experiment. I'd have brought him along, but he's an observant Jew.'

"I know about the Jewish holidays," Slaughter said. "I was a lawyer in New York, and on Yom Kippur New York's practically closed down. Too many Jews."

He corrected the slip smoothly. "I was brought up religiously

also. Too much so. 'Pleasure for man is in the hereafter.' My
father was a Calvinist. Very poor, but when I said I liked the
soup, he poured water into it. He didn't sanction the pleasures
of this world. Not even gay colors, like a loud tie or a striped
shirt. I thought I rebelled, but look at me now: gray suit, gray
tie, gray socks. I still have that old religion in my bones. I still
feel guilty when I miss church."

Cory watched him with a smile that hid his thoughts. Conditioned reflex, he concluded. It was in Slaughter's makeup to
stress that he was a churchgoer the moment religion was
mentioned. Going to church projected a reliable, trustworthy
image. The RNA molecules of religious upbringing. Also RNA
molecules of anti-Semitism, created by environment and tra-
dition.

Slaughter looked at his watch, breaking the sudden silence
between them. "Any moment now," he said.

"I'll have to leave soon. It's getting dark," Cory said, watching the quickly fading daylight.

"Well, you only want to take a look at our volunteer and ask
him a few questions. That shouldn't take long." Slaughter came
to the point that was bothering him. "Maybe I could answer
them?"

"I'm afraid not," Cory said.

"Why not enlighten me?" Slaughter pressed on. We both have
the same objective, don't we?"

"Hardly."

Slaughter smiled amicably. It was a mistake to be insistent;
people get obstinate.

"I'm not anxious, only curious."

The telephone rang. Slaughter picked it up instantly. "Send
them over," he said.

"Them?" Cory asked. "How many volunteers have you got?"

"Only one, but a safe one. Let me warn you, he isn't very
communicative."

"You seem to enjoy mysteries," Cory said.

"It's part of my profession and my training. An unnecessary word can turn into a misunderstanding and produce complications. Words one doesn't say, one doesn't need to take back."

"You seem to treat your job like a game."

"That's part of the enjoyment in life, playing a dangerous game. Don't you do the same, only more so, Doctor? You with your prying into the mysteries of nature. You're searching for a nigger in a tunnel. He might have a club in his hand."

"I told you I'm not ready to conduct that experiment."

Slaughter looked up sharply. "Don't tell me you won't go through with it."

"I haven't promised anything." Cory put his glass on the table; he had scarcely touched the drink.

There was a knock at the door, and Slaughter opened it quickly. Two men entered. One was small and sallow-faced, the other big-chested but pale.

"Mr. Foster, Mr. Alden," Slaughter murmured. "This is Dr. Cory. Please sit down."

Cory looked at Alden's thick-soled shoes and coarse hand-knit socks. His clothes were too heavy for the California sun. The other man's clothes did not fit properly. The shirt collar was too big, the gray suit old-fashioned and too wide in the shoulders; the trousers had the clownish-looking cuffs of the thirties, the tie did not match.

"Mr. Foster is eager to volunteer for your experiment. Aren't you, Foster?" Slaughter said benevolently, bending forward and fixing the man hypnotically with his eyes.

The sallow man nodded. There was a deadness about him, a lack of reaction, as if he were under the influence of a drug.

"What made you decide to volunteer?" Cory asked. He had realized at once that he was talking to a prisoner and that the heavyset man beside him was the jailer. The ill-fitting clothes had come from the prison wardrobe. The pallid skin had seen too little sunshine for too long a time.

"I want to do my share for humanity," Foster recited.

"You see," Slaughter said with satisfaction, "there are still people who are unselfish and interested in mankind. You want a drink, Foster?"

"No, thank you," the sallow man answered. "I haven't had one in twenty years. I don't think I'd like to start now." He smiled wanly, as if at a joke.

"You, Alden?"

"I'm on duty," Alden said.

Slaughter nodded and poured himself a carefully measured ounce.

Cory turned to Foster. "I assume you have been told about the experiment." He felt a sudden pity for this collapsed heap of humanity.

"Yes."

Probably he had been coached in what to say and how to act, Cory thought. Slaughter confirmed the suspicion.

"Sure he knows. Now, Alden, I think you can take Foster back to the station."

At once Alden got up.

"One moment," Cory said. "It's my duty to tell you, Mr. Foster, that this kind of experiment has not been performed on humans before."

"I know," Foster answered, turning his washed-out eyes to Cory.

"An untried experiment contains unknown components," Cory continued. "But I must warn you that your system might react violently against the injections we will give you."

"I guess that's a chance I'll have to take," he muttered. Alden and Slaughter nodded, as if they had cued the answer.

"There's also a chance of complications that might prove fatal," Cory went on.

"Now, now," Slaughter interfered. "He isn't going to die."

Foster stared at Cory. "I don't want to die," he said in a dull voice, but his face was contorted.

"Of course you won't." Slaughter had raised his voice. "That's the trouble with doctors; they exaggerate. Just to be on the safe side they bring up things that haven't got a chance in a million of happening."

"I don't want to die," the man repeated dully.

"I told you there's no chance of that," Slaughter said, controlling his anger and frustration. "Now, Alden, take him outside."

Foster turned to Cory. "Are you sure I won't die?"

"Most likely not. But I can't guarantee the outcome. As I told you, the experiment hasn't been attempted before."

"I won't go through with it," Foster said suddenly. "I don't want to die."

"See what you've done, Cory!" Slaughter's voice was low and menacing. "You scared this man quite unnecessarily. Of course he won't die. I accept the responsibility."

Foster looked at Cory as though only he and Cory were in the room. He did not plead or question; his voice was matter-of-fact.

"I don't want to die," he repeated. "I killed my wife, Doc; that was twenty years ago. I was going to be fried. I waited in the death row for two years. Then I was reprieved. I don't want to go through that agony again. I won't sign away my own life."

"But you won't, damn it!" Slaughter shouted. "You volunteered and we brought you from Sing Sing. All the way to California! Your time will be cut for your services and soon you'll be a free man. Doesn't that appeal to you? Or do you want to go back behind bars for the rest of your life?"

The man had sunk back into apathy. "You can't force me. I'm being punished for my crime. You can't condemn me to death. Nobody can."

Slaughter glared at Cory furiously.

"Let me put some sense into him, Mr. Slaughter," Alden said. "I know how to talk to these boys."

"No. I'm going to get him back to his senses." Slaughter put his half-empty glass back on the table and opened the bedroom door. "Come on, let's have a talk."

"It's useless," Cory said. "I couldn't accept that man, since he doesn't want to go through with it. Even if he changed his mind."

"Do I have to convince you too? Of course he'll go through with it."

"I don't want to die," Foster repeated, and stepped into the bedroom. Slaughter followed him and closed the door.

"I could've told you," Alden said derisively. "They all have big ideas, but when it comes time to deliver, they get cold feet. I wouldn't have told him, Doc. Why scare him off?"

His voice was hoarse and husky. Longingly he eyed the bottles. "I need one after all," he said questioningly.

"I don't think Mr. Slaughter would mind."

Alden poured himself a generous drink and swallowed it with one gulp. Then he wiped the glass with a paper napkin and held it against the light, looking for smudges.

"First they kill, and when it's their turn to pay off, they scream about injustice and capital punishment. You know, Foster hacked his wife to pieces. Carved her up like a butcher a cow, put her in little sacks. and dropped them overboard from the Staten Island Ferry, sack by sack. You know, Doc"—he put the glass back beside the bottles, his breath wafting to Cory like a visible cloud— "you know who's the prisoner and who's the jailer? Have you ever thought of that? Me, I'm the prisoner. Foster has a hell of a good time in his cell, with his radio, his books. He knows where his next meal's coming from. No worries. But me, every morning I check in I'm a prisoner. Making the rounds, I have to push a key in a hole in the wall every five minutes. That's twelve times an hour. Down there at the control panel a light flashes on, telling them where I am. I can't even go to the can without them knowing it. And I do that for hours, every day, for years."

Alden's eyes had the same blank gaze as Foster's, a stare directed vaguely at something to one side of Cory.

"I'm telling you, when I took that job I thought I'd be Simon Legree, swing the big whip. I haven't even got a nightstick. I'm the prisoner."

He listened for a moment to Slaughter's voice, which came muted from the bedroom.

"I can't even quit or I'd lose my pension. I'm in for life, Doc." Again he listened. "Why plead with that guy? Stick a needle in his ass and knock him out. Do whatever you want with him. Don't ask him. They ain't human! They should've fried him twenty years ago. Just think of the taxpayers' money, yours and mine, he's cost. Man. I'm holding onto the wrong end of the stick!"

The bedroom door opened. Slaughter appeared, his face dark. He went quickly to the array of bottles and poured bourbon into a glass, then found the bourbon he had left on the table and slowly poured one into the other. Foster stood in the doorway, his face ashen, his eyes without focus. With a slow movement of his thin neck, he turned to Cory; his Adam's apple jerked convulsively.

"Take him back, Alden," Slaughter said disgustedly. "He'll never get out of Sing Sing if I can help it."

"I could've told you," Alden said. "None of those guys ever stick to their promises. They can kill but they're yellow. There isn't a bigger coward than a murderer. Come on, Foster."

The prisoner walked to the door, his shoulders hunched. Alden grabbed him roughly.

"I hoped to stay in California for a few days. I was looking forward to it. This is the first time I've been out West and you've spoiled it."

"Get him out of here fast," Slaughter grunted.

Both men left, trailing the stale smell of jail and mothballs.

"Satisfied?' Slaughter asked Cory, baring his long teeth. He lit a cigarette. "What do we do next?"

"You would've preferred me not to warn that man?" Cory said.

"He is a murderer."

"He is a living person and must be told about the consequences of this experiment. You failed to do that."

"Where do we get our man?"

"I can't answer that."

"Where can we dig up somebody on this short notice? You've got a list of people. We could pick one from that."

Cory walked to the door. "I told you I'm not fully prepared for the test."

"If we had the trepidation you scientists have, believe me, this country would be in a mess."

"I have to leave," Cory said, his hand on the doorknob.

"Good *yom tov*," Slaughter said.

4

"You should've been at my father's house after *neilah*," Hillel said, resettling a skullcap on his thick black hair. "You'd have thought you were back in a fourteenth-century Spanish ghetto."

"The *neilah is* the closing service of Yom Kippur," Karen shouted from the kitchen. "Hillel, don't smother the Dottore with your Hebrew knowledge." (Once Cory had had an Italian assistant who called him Dottore, and the name had stuck.)

The small apartment smelled of roasted fowl. On a thin, old, handwoven cloth stood a baccarat carafe filled with wine. The table was laid for three with silver knives and forks. Crystal glasses reflected the candlelight, and the candles were stuck into an amazing variety of containers: pottery, silver candlesticks, even small colored glasses.

A smile lighted Hillel's thin, dark face. Cory had never seen him so relaxed. But neither had he ever seen him harassed, brooding, preoccupied with his thoughts; in complete balance and in complete control of his emotions, he never seemed bothered by insoluble scientific problems.

Hillel went into the kitchen, and a moment later Cory heard Karen laugh. "Get out of here! There's a time and a place for everything!"

Hillel appeared, smiling cheerfully. "My father would never have kissed his wife in the kitchen. Kissing one's wife on Yom Kippur—he would have been horrified!"

"This guy is oversexed," Karen shouted from around the corner. "That's why I married him."

Hillel lit some candles floating in oil.

"Every day is a new day." he said. "That's the beauty of life; every day we can start from scratch. But we Jews are fatalists. On Rosh Hashanah, the fate for the year is inscribed in the tablets of heaven. On Yom Kippur, the Day of Atonement, it is sealed, and after that it will not be changed."

"Then you believe in predestination?" Cory asked. He knew that Hillel's faith did not influence his scientific thinking. It was a thing apart from his profession. He knew him to be level-headed, intelligent, hard-working, and extremely quick-minded. There was a rapport between them. Cory rarely needed to finish a sentence, Hillel had grasped its meaning beforehand.

"We Jews were saying *'Que sera, sera'* long before the Spaniards spoke Spanish," Hillel said.

He was pouring the wine when Karen appeared from the kitchen carrying a soup tureen on a silver tray. "Light some more candles, please, Dottore," she said. "Everybody should do something constructive on the Day of Atonement."

"I don't know what sins I have to atone for," Cory said, but he obeyed. "Sinning takes time, and I don't have any to spare. I'm three years behind in my work and eight years behind in sinning."

He felt the outside world retreat pleasantly into the distance. Slaughter seemed unreal, and even the campus had faded from his mind.

Karen switched off the electric light in the kitchen bathing the small living room in candlelight. It accented Karen's round forehead, the widely spaced eyes, the generous mouth. Hillel and Karen seemed to him to have been born in the wrong century; they could have been Phoenicians, perhaps, or Egyptians, descendants of the pharaohs, a prince and princess inbred to an ultimate fineness, the last of their line. They looked like brother and sister, joined in an incestuous marriage. Their perfect understanding left no room for intrusion from outsiders, not even for children. Hillel and Karen shared secret jokes which eluded Cory; still he felt they accepted him.

"Today I'll have a little wine," Hillel the teetotaler announced, lifting his goblet, and he drank to Karen and Cory. "This is the highest Sabbath, on Yom Kippur. One lives from Sabbath to Sabbath. The days of the week fall into place around Sabbath. Wednesday, Thursday and Friday are 'before Sabbath,' Sunday, Monday, and Tuesday are 'after Sabbath,' and they receive holiness from the Sabbath that is past."

"Don't listen to him," Karen said. "He only talks that way once a year. On all the other Sabbaths he brings back his homework. *L'chayim!*" she toasted Cory. There was a mocking spark in her dark eyes. Hillel looked as he must have when he first fell in love with her.

"Will you join us in a prayer?" he asked.

"Do you expect him to object?" Karen said.

"Baruch atah adonay elohey-nu melech ha-olam asher kid-sha-no b'mits-vo-tav b'tsi-ca-no l'had'lik ner shel yom tov," he chanted in Hebrew, swaying his body back and forth.

"Now we can eat; the soup's getting cold," Karen said. "I cook well only once a year, so please appreciate it. Generally Hillel doesn't know what he's putting in his mouth. Good food is wasted on him."

"I wasn't spoiled at home," Hillel said. "Besides, it didn't matter what one ate during the week. All good things were kept for Sabbath."

Karen dipped thick soup from the tureen.

"I had a visitor from Washington," Cory said, unable to keep the problem to himself any longer.

Karen looked at Cory pleadingly. "This is our day of rest and yours too, Dottore. Mental rest, I mean. I forbade Hillel even to *think* of work. And he promised me not to. Hillel, did you think?" She bent forward and squinted at him. He put his hand on hers, and Cory felt like an intruder.

"I didn't dare use my head today," Hillel said. "But you aren't being much of a hostess. Maybe what the Dottore has to tell us has nothing to do with work. Give him a chance."

Karen again looked warningly at Cory.

"It is business," Cory confessed. "We won't talk about it to-night. The case is closed."

"What case?"

"Don't!" Karen insisted. Framed by long eyelashes and heavy eyebrows, her irises looked slightly outward; her face had a childlike innocence and vulnerability.

Hillel lifted his hand in submission. "Okay, I won't."

At that moment the telephone rang.

"I bet it's his mother," Karen said. "She's afraid her son, having fasted a whole day, might have perished from starvation."

Hillel picked up the telephone. "For you." he said. handing Cory the receiver.

It was Slaughter.

"I finally got you." His voice rang with suppressed fury, as if Cory were deliberately hiding from him. "At the campus they refused to give out Mondoro's number, and he isn't listed in the directory. What is he, some picture star? Even the President of the United States you can reach, but not a lousy chemist!"

"Well, what is it?" Cory asked, annoyed. "You found the number."

"I had to get it from Washington," Slaughter complained. Hillel must be in Slaughter's files too. Cory felt he had walked into a well-prepared net.

"Our man is in a coma."

"He's been in a coma for days, you told me," Cory said. "And I told you not to count on me."

"You'd better come over right away and start working on him. Bring your chemist. I'm at the Medical Center on campus. At Dr. Queen's office. Got him on Yom Kippur. He isn't a Jew."

"There's nothing I can do or want to do," Cory said, raising his voice against his will to match Slaughter's.

"Oh, yes, you will! Get over here and dig up a volunteer for us. We'll never have a chance like this again."

"Impossible. You know my objections." Cory glanced at Karen and Hillel who were pretending not to listen.

"They don't interest me," Slaughter rasped savagely. "Here, Queen, you talk to him. He doesn't understand what's at stake. I can't get through to him."

"Slaughter..."

But Dr. Queen was already on the line, his usually flat voice full of excitement. "Cory, Mr. Slaughter told me about that experiment you have in mind."

"I don't have anything in mind. Besides, it can't be done on such short notice."

"This man here is dying of uremia. We could put his brain in nitrogen and keep it deep-frozen for a few hours until you're ready."

"I can't go through with it. You know yourself it's no good starting any experiment without being completely prepared. I could only do half of it, and then what?"

"I won't leave the Center until I hear from you." Queen hung up.

"Sorry," Cory said, turning back to the table.

"I'll bring the goose," Karen said. "Have you ever had goose Polish, Dottore?"

Cory did not answer. She went into the kitchen.

"How did Queen get into the act?" Hillel asked.

Karen took out the soup plates and put a huge silver goose-laden dish on the table. "Here, Hillel, the carving knife."

Her eyes did not leave Cory's as Hillel carved the sizzling bird.

"When we chose our profession," he said, cutting as expertly as a surgeon, "we forged our chains. We might kid ourselves into believing in free will. But we're behind bars. Our profession is our life. The inside of an answer is a joy, and the symmetry of the universe that embraces the atom and the galaxies is beautiful."

"Please," Karen said. "Is there nothing in life except work?"

"White or dark?" Hillel asked, and without waiting for a reply put part of the bird on Cory's plate. "Research never for-
gives you if you desert it for a moment. You have to think of it
constantly. If you ever cut the fine thread, you might never be
able to knot both ends together again. Please help yourself to
the cabbage, Dottore."

He served Karen and sat down.

"The Germans have a word for it, I believe. They call it
Selbstzweck, a thing self-contained. Work is *Selbstzweck.* When
I first watched you, Dottore, I couldn't understand your devotion to your work. But you've taught me. There's only one way
to succeed—your way."

"Please," Karen said unhappily, "this is Yom Kippur, the one
day you must take a night off. You're having a holiday dinner
with the Dottore and me. It wasn't cooked on a Bunsen burner."

Hillel put down his knife and fork. His darkly hand some
face looked searchingly at Cory. "You were offered the RNA of
a dying man. You refused."

"You know as well as I do that we're not prepared."

"Why wait? We could have a brain that might still be alive.
We can't throw away that chance. I'm twenty-eight, Dottore,
and you know what bothers me? The time that has already
gone by, past and irretrievable. I haven't accomplished enough.
We should never sleep, never marry, never make love, never
read anything except the literature of our work."

"He wants a divorce," Karen said. "Never make love? Is there
anything more important than that?"

Hillel put his hand on hers, but talked to Cory.

"Let's go over to the Medical Center right away," he said.

"Why?" Karen asked. "Other opportunities will come along.
Sad as this case sounds, it isn't unique."

"It is," Cory said. "In this case, it is."

He got up and picked up the telephone. "Sorry, Karen," he said as he dialed, "but there are ramifications in this case I can't talk about ... Queen? How's the situation? ... Stimulate his heart. Even if you think he's dead, keep him on the kidney machine. I'll be over in a few minutes."

Hillel got up. Karen sat motionless.

"What a dinner! Am I his wife? I wonder. He doesn't even need a housekeeper. He wouldn't bother making his bed; he'd forget to eat. If it were another girl I could fight, but how can you fight a centrifuge?"

"Sorry, Karen," Cory said. "Hillel will stay here with you. I can manage with Queen."

"Not a chance," Hillel said. "You heard her, she understands." He hugged and kissed her, lifting her off her feet, but the gesture was hurried and unconvincing.

"I'll send him home in an hour," Cory said, but he avoided her eyes.

5

Cory saw Karl Hauser's face only once, in the Medical Center's operating room. It was that of a middle-aged man in his early fifties, perhaps, with high Slavic cheekbones, the skin around his chin hanging flabbily, as though he had once been fat and had lost a great deal of weight. His body below the rib cage was sunken, giving him something of a hermaphroditic shape.

"Look at this," Queen said, uncovering him. "He's been mutilated, and very crudely. I bet they did that in a concentration camp. I've never seen such butchery. It's a miracle he survived."

"He's not a Jew," Hillel said. "What is he? A Russian? A Pole?"

"He's German," Cory said. Queen covered the body with the sheet.

The vaulted bones of the skull, the high forehead depressed at the temples, dominated the small face below. The head was partly bald; the mouth was sensual, soft and small. It was a face put together out of odds and ends, the face of a man torn by life.

"His body must've changed in the last few years," Cory said. "Also his character. Castration changes the metabolism. This was a very desperate man."

Hauser's eyes were open but without focus. Cory watched him breathe but did not know if the man's breast muscles moved voluntarily or if it was caused by the air forced into his lungs by the heart-lung machine.

The figure on the operating table, bathed in the green light reflected from the green-tiled walls, might have been a large animal or an inanimate object. The three men were alone. There were no assistants or nurses. This was not an operation but an experiment conducted in silence, without witnesses, sanctioned by the mysterious purpose of a government office.

"Exsanguination would minimize the likelihood of bleeding into the skull while the brain is being removed," Cory said, wrapping his green gown around him more securely.

Queen looked up. He wore large, myopic-looking glasses which covered most of his face between skullcap and green gauze mask. He was a small man with fast, birdlike movements, trained to work at great speed on the perishable matter under his scalpel.

"We can't do that. If the cerebral circulation is interrupted, anoxia will affect the deeper parts of the brain."

"We'll have to freeze it completely in nitrogen. *In toto.* It works on ox brains. It might work here. What's the time required for freezing?"

He turned to Hillel, who at once covered a Dewar vessel with a cloth and rolled its stand closer to the table on which the body lay. "Fifteen seconds for an animal not weighing more than a hundred grams. That multiplied by fourteen would approximate this man's brain."

"That'd be three and a half minutes," Cory computed. "Too long. We must try the freezing process while still giving artificial respiration."

"Freezing disturbs the pulmonary respiration," Queen said, studying the etiolated face on the table. "I'd better insert a tracheal cannula."

"In animal tests the heart still beats strongly after the brain has been completely iced. That would happen in this case also. The heart seems to function apart from the brain."

"Clinically, this man is dead," Queen said. "If we stopped the heart pump, there'd be nothing left to call life."

"And how much is left now?"

"I can't answer that. But if he were a hospital case, I'd close the book on him," Queen said with finality.

Cory pursed his lips thoughtfully. "We could measure the

brain's temperature during the freezing with thermocouples implanted at different depths."

"I'll do whatever you say," Queen answered. "This is your case. not mine."

"The best way is to submerge the whole head in liquid nitrogen at a temperature below minus one hundred eighty degrees," Cory said at last. "That would prevent the cerebellum and brain stem from being damaged. There would be no bleeding and no disturbance of the cerebral cortex."

"I've got the Dewar flask filled with four liters of liquid nitrogen, enough to submerge the whole head," Hillel interjected.

Cory turned toward the window separating the observation room from the operating theater. There stood Slaughter, transfixed, listening to their voices over a loudspeaker. He turned and put a handkerchief to his mouth, suppressing a bout of retching, and hastily left the room.

"All I can say is that this man is dead and that these visible functions are machine-induced. I want to be on record on that, Cory. This is a postmortem for me."

"You certainly don't need me for the rest of this operation," Cory said. "You know better than I what to do."

"I'm not so sure of that," Queen said nervously. "If that man from Washington hadn't flashed those credentials, I wouldn't have touched this case."

Cory took off his mask and rubber gloves.

"I'll be in my office, Hillel. Call me there."

"In an hour or so," Hillel answered.

Cory left. He knew he could trust Queen with the rest of the operation, a mechanical procedure based on skill, routine, repeated a thousand times on animals: cutting into the skull with the Gigli saw, quickly slicing through the skin and muscles of the neck with the scalpel—skillful incisions made with knowing ease.

Slaughter was waiting for him outside the Medical Center,

standing motionless in a cloud of wind-blown leaves "I couldn't take it," he said as Cory came up to him. "I've seen men die, but never like that."

"There's no proof that he was still alive. But you should have stayed. You missed a good show," Cory said with deliberate cruelty. "Queen will open the skull, exposing the cortex, sever the spinal and sensory connections, pour liquid nitrogen over the cortex, and lift out the brain after chipping away various tissues around the cerebellum. Then he'll put the brain into the liquid nitrogen."

Slaughter swallowed convulsively. "I wouldn't make a good medic."

"One gets used to anything."

The biochemistry building was dark except for a couple of lights burning on the staircase. As they went up the stairs to Cory's office, Slaughter put his hand against the wall to steady himself. Cory unlocked the door and turned on the lights. The fluorescent tubes threw an unhealthy glare over their shadowy faces.

Slaughter slumped into a chair. "What's the next step, Cory?"

"Extracting the RNA."

"Where do we find the volunteer?"

"Foster was the wrong guinea pig. He'd never have been able to coordinate his thoughts and express them clearly. Certainly not for our purpose. We need somebody who has had training in chemistry and biochemistry and who knows how to interpret experiments, not a man whose brain has been burned out after twenty years of vegetating in a prison."

"Then even if I were to volunteer I'd be unsuitable—"

"Not as bad as Foster, but certainly not ideal."

The cigarette between Slaughter's fingers had burned down to his stained nails. He lit another one.

"You're a brave man, Cory."

"I?"

"I'm getting an inside look into your character that isn't in the file. You're thinking of trying out his RNA on yourself!"

"How did you come to that conclusion?"

"Obvious, isn't it? You know exactly how much danger there will be in this case. You know how to counteract unfavorable reactions. You've made hundreds of animal tests. And the reports from Sweden and Canada so far haven't mentioned a single fatality."

"The RNA they used on humans was extracted from yeast. The major side effects were nausea and vomiting, a drop in blood pressure, fever, and hyperventilation. We don't know if a human system will accept human RNA, though I expect that RNA of the same species is less toxic than that of a foreign species. In fact, the reaction to human RNA might be no more violent than the reaction to yeast RNA. But all this is assumption. We have no empirical tests."

Slaughter grinned. He knew how to close the trap Cory had laid for himself. "There must be a point in research where assumptions have to be proven by empirical tests, to use your own words, Dr. Cory."

Cory did not answer. He got up. "Let's take a walk over to the chemistry building. Mondoro should show up soon. Let's hear what he has to say."

6

The smell of formalin and cleaning solution permeated the air of the big laboratory in the chemistry building. The room was partitioned with high wooden walls. In the compartments between them small motors ran, ticked, hummed, moving levers and tiny wheels, pressing air into bubbling liquids, activating flashing lights in boxes, turning numbered counters. Slaughter had no idea what these custom-made contraptions were for, but his tiredness and depression were gone. He found himself within an organization: file cabinets, typewriters, telephones, desks covered with books and papers. This was home to him. People who create organizations arrive at concrete results; he called it Slaughter's Law.

He watched a medium-sized, olive-faced young man wheel up a dolly on which stood a contraption that looked like a giant vacuum cleaner.

"Dr. Mondoro," Cory said. "Mr. Slaughter, from Washington."

The young man lifted the container onto a table already cluttered with machines, vessels, and blown-glass flasks.

"You phoned Dr. Cory at my home," Hillel said.

"Sorry to have disturbed your Yom Kippur."

"It's all right."

Hillel was putting a large empty stainless-steel vessel on the table. As he started to unscrew the top of the vacuum container, Cory said, "You'd better go home. I promised Karen to keep you only an hour. She'll sue for divorce and name me as co-respondent."

"I called her from the Center. She understands," Hillel said cheerfully. "You marry an understanding woman or you don't marry at all. How does your wife bear up, Mr. Slaughter, when you don't come home for dinner or run away as soon as you've eaten?"

"She's used to it," Slaughter said. "As it happens, she gets nervous when I'm home too often."

He was uncomfortable. The smells in the building bothered him. The air was filled with a peculiar odor of preservatives. The vacuum container on the table hid something terrifying. Slaughter had once seen a play in which a murderer carried around a hatbox containing the severed head of his victim. He didn't like the sight of blood.

Hillel removed the clamps retaining the lid.

"I suggest we treat it like the ox brain," Cory said.

"Well, we don't know any other method, do we?"

"You don't need to close your eyes," Cory said maliciously. "It's the blood that shocks most people, not the shape of the thing. It won't look any worse than a piece of brain in a super-market."

Slaughter forced a smile. "I'm tired, I guess."

The thing Hillel was holding in the forceps was waxy pink and looked like a plastic replica of a brain. He dropped it back into the stainless-steel vessel.

Slaughter made a desperate joke. "Now I'm sure he's dead."

"Whatever's in this gray matter might be very much alive," Cory answered, twisting the knife.

Slaughter suddenly yearned for the seclusion of his bunga-low, a nightcap, and bed.

"I thought you'd be curious to see how such an experiment is conducted, for your report to Washington," Cory said smoothly. "We wouldn't be working on this if you hadn't asked us to."

"They'll never believe the report," said Slaughter gloomily. "It's all too fantastic. Even if they saw it happening"—Suddenly he came in alive. "I'd like to call my superiors and get them to come out here," he said formally. "They'll have to see for them-selves."

"You can call from here. There's a phone," Cory said. Slaughter detected a sarcastic undertone.

Shielding his hand from Cory's and Hillel's eyes, he dialed a number. "There won't be any charge on this call ... Six-eighty ... Get me Colonel Borg." He put his hand over the mouthpiece. "It's only fair that my boss keep the same working hours.... Slaughter speaking. Yes, I know it's three in the morning where you are, but I'd like to suggest that you and Dr. Wendtland come out here right away. An emergency came up. I can't explain on the phone. First plane after twelve Pacific time? I'll be at the airport. Good night, sir."

He hung up, relief in his eyes. Cory was watching him with a sardonic smile.

"I want a written release that I'm performing this experiment at the request of the government."

"My friends from Washington will give it to you." Slaughter sympathized. Never accept responsibility if you can shift it to somebody else.

He grinned with satisfaction as Mondoro opened a big refrigerator and put in the vessel with its pinkish content. The door closed, locking in Hauser's memory and its secrets.

7

"Slaughter." Hillel turned the word in his mouth as if it were a substance. "Slaughter—the name fits him. His ancestors must've been butchers, or hangmen, masked people torturing prisoners with hot irons."

"Savage, Slaughter, Killer—good Anglo-Saxon names." Cory was brewing coffee in the little kitchen in his apartment. He poured it into the saucerless mugs standing on the kitchen table. "You're acquiring bad habits from me not going to sleep. That's only for bachelors."

Hillel warmed his hands on the mug. "Karen accuses you of making me over in your image, Dottore. I wish I had your scientific imagination. Then I wouldn't want to put my brain to sleep either."

"You have an important compensation in Karen."

Cory sat down opposite him. The small apartment was bland and impersonal. Only books gave it life, books on stands, piled on the floor, on tables, heaped upon each other; and papers, scribbled notes strewn all over the room.

"Karen. I really don't deserve her."

"But your marriage is exceptionally happy."

"That's her doing, not mine. She understands me better than I do myself. She heaps so much love and protection on me that I take them for granted. She's spoiled me rotten." Hillel stared at his mug for a moment. "I feel guilty about not doing enough for her."

"Have children, and she'll have to share her love."

"That might be the solution—keeping her perpetually pregnant. But will I find time for my children? She might not forgive me then.... You understand, Dottore. You remember how it was before your wife died." He knew he could always speak forthrightly to Cory.

"It wasn't like your marriage. I felt strangled," Cory said with uncharacteristic intensity. "I'm a loner. I know I'm deficient of emotions that come naturally to other human beings. I'm a scientist by compulsion, not by choice. Faced with a problem that interests me, I stop thinking humanly. That's why I never had friends—I can only cope with demands in my profession." He checked himself. "What I'm really doing is just catering to my own curiosity. This is my objective in life—acquiring more knowledge. And by doing so I sacrifice human emotions. More coffee?"

Hillel locked his fingers around his mug. "Humanity's going to benefit more from you than from any other living scientist, Dottore. Great men are always monomaniacs and loners. Everyone is looking for immortality. In a sense you have already achieved it."

"Does it really matter if people remember you after you're dead? Only what we experience consciously is important. It doesn't do Michelangelo or Dante a bit of good that people still marvel at their genius and admire their work. Nor does it help men like Van Gogh, who died before knowing his paintings would be valuable. Wanting to achieve immortality is the ultimate conceit. Most people care only about themselves. Take Slaughter, for example. What does he want? I guess he's jockeying for position, using us against people in Washington. He told them all you have to do is transfer RNA from one person to another for the recipient to inherit the donor's memory and reveal all the secrets the dead man had stored up in his cortex. I don't think he even believes in his own scheme, but that's what he has sold to his superiors in Washington. If it doesn't work out, we'll have failed, not he."

"What secrets?"

"I don't know." Cory shrugged.

"But who's going to be the receiver of the RNA?" Hillel said eagerly. "I haven't met him yet."

"Slaughter brought a man along, some poor convict they'd virtually blackmailed by promising him anything to make him comply. They got him from prison and would've sent him back as soon as he completed the test. That is, if he survived the experiment."

"A prisoner? Clever! I thought we weren't allowed to work on human guinea pigs. Where is he?"

"He backed out. He didn't want to die."

"There is that chance."

A clock in the adjoining room chimed two o'clock. Cory moved restlessly in his chair. "We won't have any positive proof that human memory-transfer works until we've tested it on humans."

"But where can we find a man who'll volunteer?"

"Slaughter made a valid suggestion."

"Is he going to volunteer? I'd admire him for it."

"He put it to me that I should. I told him that the receiver of the RNA should be a trained psychologist, a biochemist, someone who's able to communicate his experience."

"You?" Hillel's head snapped up in horror.

"I'm contemplating it. Of course, I couldn't carry out the experiment without your help. You're acquainted with the tests. We'd be a good team. The best!"

"And what if the procedure proves fatal?"

"Then, of course, the experiment will have failed. But it could also succeed, couldn't it?"

"How could you ever consider such an idea, Dottore!"

"It isn't such a farfetched idea, Hillel. It makes sense Besides, my curiosity's the strongest thing about me."

"If we should lose you on account of it, Dottore ... No ... it's inconceivable. What about your future contributions to science? Dozens of people could do the experiment. Why you?"

"I'm the best qualified. You know, since I told you about the idea, I'm more determined than ever to go through with it.

We've worked too long in the dark. Our experiments with RNA are mostly conjecture. Maybe this one will tell us the answer."

"No!" Hillel burst out desperately, but checked himself at once. He relaxed, and smiled. "I haven't the right to stop you. The only right I have is to venture my opinion. Sorry."

"You're talking sense." Cory got up and put the mugs in the sink. "I'm counting on your help," he said as he walked Hillel to the door.

"Good night, Dottore. Or, rather, good morning."

Cory opened the door. Hillel turned, as if he were going to say something important, but he only repeated "Good night" and left.

Cory undressed in his spartan bedroom—a low narrow bed, a Danish chest, one chair, no rugs on the floor— then went into the bathroom to douse himself with cold water. He would permit himself to sleep for three hours; then, refreshed, he would weigh the value of being a guinea pig for the RNA experiment.

Hillel opened the door to his apartment as quietly as he could, remembering the tiny squeak the unoiled hinges made. The squeak came, and at once he heard Karen's voice from the bedroom.

"Hillel?"

He suddenly realized how tired he was. The last few hours' tension had worn him out. He threw his coat on a chair in the living room and stretched hard. Then he walked into the bedroom, undressing as he went, absently letting his clothes lie where they dropped.

Karen was in bed, a book on the sheet, her dark hair framing her face, her eyes big and moist.

"I forgot how late it was," Hillel muttered. He always felt as guilty as if he had neglected her deliberately.

"I knew," she said, folding her thin tanned arms behind her neck and letting the half-open book slide onto the carpet. "But if I wait for you one minute—it's one minute lost!" She intended it as an extravagant joke, but it came out sounding serious.

"We worked, and then I went to Cory's for a cup of coffee." Hillel threw off his shirt. His olive-skinned body was muscular, narrow at the hips. Karen watched him with pleasure, the play of his back muscles, the narrow buttocks, as he stepped into the bathroom.

"Don't turn on the shower. You'll wake up the neighbors."

"You're just saying that to get me to bed faster."

As soon as he slid into the bed she rolled over toward him. "I'm jealous of your work. I want your work to be me." She turned out the light.

Hillel stared at the wall. As his eyes grew used to the dark, the faint glow of a night light slowly appeared.

Whenever he wanted to sleep, he hypnotized himself with the light.... Cory. What a crazy idea, sacrificing himself for the experiment. Obviously he was determined to go through with it. There had to be a way to stop him.

"What are you thinking about?" Karen said, moving her foot until it found his.

"About you." Hillel turned and kissed her. "How can I think of anything else when you're so close?"

"Ah," she sighed, framing his face with her hands. "Now you're talking the way I like you to talk. I know I'm too possessive. But what else can I do, being in love with you?"

He tightened his arms. "No woman can be too possessive when she's in bed with a man, not even if he's her own husband."

She laughed.

8

Slaughter walked down the long gangway leading to the arrival area at the International Airport in Inglewood. A moving band ran under his feet, but he strode past the people who were standing still and letting themselves be carried along. He wore his blue London suit, ordered from an advertisement in an English magazine. He liked to give the impression of being an Englishman on his way to his office. Besides, being formally dressed was protection against the disturbingly unconventional Californians.

A dulcet female voice announced the arrival of the Washington plane. Slaughter, as always, was on time. He looked around for the best place to watch for Borg and Wendtland.

Wendtland was easy to spot, with his scarred, flat-cheeked face. Once, in a fit of amiability, he explained to Slaughter how he had got the cut in his cheek fighting a duel with sabers, and had put a piece of thin wire into the cut to make a scar. Scars were class symbols in those days. Wendtland was rescued by the American forces from the concentration camp he had been sent to for his part in the anti-Hitler plot, and became one of their advisers in German civil affairs. Then he was invited to enter the Secret Service. Now he was head of a special department of the CIA, an expert on Eastern Germany. Tall and lean, very erect, Wendtland walked fast and a small step ahead of Borg, a stubby, round-faced man in casual clothes, as usual generating his chosen air of cheerful good-fellowship.

"Hi, Francis," Borg yelled, jovially slapping Slaughter's shoulder. Wendtland only nodded a greeting.

They joined the stream of arriving travelers. "I've got room for you in my bungalow," Slaughter said. "It's quite comfortable."

"I'm looking forward to a damn good time," said Borg. "I

haven't been out West in years."

"What's the trouble?" Wendtland cut in. He disliked small talk.

"Hauser's dead. They've frozen his brain. But we need a volunteer. Cory rejected our man."

"Then he should procure another."

"He might just do that," Slaughter said casually, lowering his voice. "I did my share to find him."

"What are you talking about?" Wendtland snapped. Impatience was one of the weapons he used to keep the people who worked for him off guard.

"I believe Cory will offer himself for the test," Slaughter said, taking all the credit.

"Excellent!" Borg playfully pushed his fist into Slaughter's side. "Your idea, Francis? It couldn't be better. We'll tell Cory what we expect of him. He's intelligent. I'm sure we'll have no trouble there."

"Quite the contrary," Wendtland interfered sharply. "We will tell him nothing. Nothing at all."

They had reached the luggage dispenser on the ground floor, which was scattering suitcases noisily in all directions.

"If he knows nothing about Hauser, every piece of information we get from him will be valid; if he invents, we'll know it. If he knows what we're after, his thought associations will be based on his knowledge of the dead man and therefore of questionable authenticity." Wendtland suddenly turned to Slaughter, his eyes two pieces of glass set in a motionless face. "How much have you told Cory?"

"All he knows is that Hauser was a defector who got shot. That's all."

"Too much. Every detail that Cory knows diminishes his value for us."

Slaughter's skin turned a blotchy white; he hated to be reprimanded. Stiffly he turned to look for his superiors' luggage.

Not until they were driving toward Beverly Hills did Wendtland loosen up. "I know Hauser from Peenemunde during the war. He worked on the V-2 missiles. At that time he was in his late twenties or early thirties, a crack mathematician and physicist. Too bad the Russians got him before the Americans could get hold of him."

"I was never told why Hauser defected," Slaughter said tentatively.

"We were in touch with him for years when he was working in that Russian atom city Baikonur. He wanted to come over to our side. He has his wife in Berlin and his son in Eastern Germany. There was a symposium in Prague, and the Russians took him over there to talk to the Czechs. We got him from Prague, to East Berlin and then across. All of a sudden he stopped being cooperative, but we needed him in Washington, so we got him out. He didn't see his wife or his son. Somehow he'd got in touch with the Russians, and when we wanted to fly him out, he got shot. The whole thing was a mess." Wendtland's face looked pinched and angry. "Bungled. I wish our organization could be as disciplined as Canaris' was. The way that man ran German counterintelligence during World War II! Compared to him, we're a bunch of amateurs." He brooded gloomily. "And now we want to transfer a dead man's memory to a living one. If that isn't a kind of insanity, I don't know what is."

"Is it, Francis?" Borg asked, delicately probing. He had already sent a secret report to Wendtland's superior objecting to the scheme.

"Cory might have the answer," Slaughter said diplomatically. "It could work, couldn't it?"

Wendtland continued to look glumly out of the window. "People have tried things that looked impossible and succeeded," he said, reassuring himself. "I'll know more after I've talked to Slaughter's witch doctor."

Slaughter had an uneasy feeling that Wendtland was trying to shift responsibility for the case onto him. Borg listened silently. He was enjoying their predicament; already he saw himself sitting in Wendtland's penthouse office.

9

"If there is a chemical formula for memory, there must be one for elation, one for fear, courage, devotion, love, hatred. Have you found the chemical components of man's soul, Dr. Cory?" Borg gibed.

It was night again in the laboratory. The big hall was empty. Hillel had taken the vessel containing Hauser's brain from the freezer, where its temperature had been raised to zero degrees Fahrenheit.

"Not yet," Cory said. "We'll get there one day So far we've been content with small achievements, like making mice attack cats and cats afraid of mice. We can control people's emotions and make them happy with pills. Just tell me what mood you want, Colonel, and I'll give you the elixir for it."

"I get my relaxation from only one source, the whiskey bottle," Borg grinned.

Before him lay a large pinkish mass wrapped in cloth, flanked by a row of labeled bottles. Hillel brought out a set of homogenizers—long, thick glass test tubes, each containing a snugly fitting plastic piston on a stainless steel shaft. The plastic was white, like a bleached bone. Wendtland put on his glasses.

"I'm grateful to you for letting us watch," he said to Cory. Casually he threw out the hook. "We have asked Mr. Slaughter to discuss a fee with you, since there are various funds available for extraordinary services."

"I told Mr. Slaughter that I'm an employee of the university not of your ... office." The sarcasm in Cory's eyes dropped into his voice. "But if you insist on making a donation to the Institute, I'm sure you won't be rebuffed, Dr. Wendtland. We are not heavily endowed. Berkeley, for instance, can put a dozen men on the job while we're struggling with two."

"Of course, of course," Wendtland said, his eyes on Hillel's hands as they unwrapped the pink brain. "The money will be submitted to the university through a neutral agency. How much do you suggest?"

"Fifty thousand would be appropriate," Cory said in an indifferent voice.

Hillel looked up sharply. So far, he had shown no interest in the conversation; Slaughter had tried and failed to catch his eye. Then Hillel bent his head and worked on, absorbed; he might have been alone in the laboratory.

"Fifty grand," Borg repeated.

Wendtland was unmoved. "If the experiment should turn out to be successful, it's a reasonable fee."

As if slicing a mortadella, Hillel carved up the gray matter, cutting off pieces of equal thickness with even, unhurried strokes, and laid them out on a block of ice. Slaughter felt his throat tighten.

"I realize, of course, that you can't guarantee anything," Wentland said in a neutral tone. "Slaughter told us that you want to carry out the experiment on yourself. I'm encouraged, Dr. Cory, by your faith in your work."

Again Hillel looked up.

Cory said nothing. Deftly he slipped a slice of brain into a homogenizer tube and added an icy solution of salt, sodium docecylsulfate, and bentonite. He decided to give them information for their money.

"You see," he said, as he pushed the stainless steel shaft of a plastic piston into the flexible coupling of a small motor. "the major technical problem is that there are many RNA's, and it's necessary to separate the carriers of memory from their close relatives, the carriers of instructions."

He stepped on a foot switch, and the plastic piston spun with sudden life. Carefully, almost lovingly, he stroked the homogenizer tube up and down the whirling piston, which forced the tissue between the walls of the glass tube and the piston shaft to be crushed and disintegrated. Soon the solution was a uniform gray, and he poured the contents into a beaker packed in ice and began again with another slice of brain tissue.

"In a sense," Cory went on, "it is as though we were giants who have to learn a message told to one Western Union boy sitting in some unknown building in a city like New York. The only way to do it is to grind up the city, as I am now doing to the marvelous architecture of this brain, and somehow devise a procedure first to separate the people from the buildings, then the boys from the girls, and finally our particular messenger boy from all the other boys. And it must all be done gently, very gently, so that our messenger boy isn't injured and his message lost."

Cory smiled bleakly before continuing.

"Everything we do is designed to this end. We extract with different solvents—phenol or a detergent to get rid of the protein, in particular the protein enzymes that destroy the RNA and decompose the message; salt to separate the memory messages from the genetic messages of the DNA by their different solubilities; and so on, at every stage refining by centrifuging, always gently, always cold."

The squat box of the centrifuge whirled away, the vacuum sucking the air out of the chamber so that the solution could be centrifuged at 100,000 rpm without generating heat, enabling the separation to take place very gently.

The three men were floating in an ocean of perplexity. Cory enjoyed their confusion for a moment.

"Of course," he went on, "at first we only spin slowly, at twenty thousand rpm, because it's easy to separate little boys from big buildings, but as our fraction gets purer and purer, the separations require narrower distinctions.

We precipitate the RNA with alcohol and then put our powder of messenger boys on a long methylated albumen Kieselguhr column, which they run down as though running down a long corridor, and we separate out only those that run fast. And then we separate them again by centrifuging them through sucrose or cesium chloride of different densities, and we put them on the column again and make them run a new race. And at the end we have obtained from this great city one-thousandth of a gram of messenger boys for every thousand grams of their weight, and of all those messenger boys only one in a thousand is what we want."

"Well, I lost you early in the lecture," Borg said, "but all I can say is, fifty thousand for the experiment is a bargain."

"Fascinating," Wendtland muttered. He was lost. Was this a conjurer's trick? A fraud? He had to allocate fifty thousand dollars of secret funds and be prepared to justify the expense. What if Cory made fools of them all? There was nothing on paper. Nothing could be proved.

"It took about thirty years to find these methods," Cory said, tipping more brain solution into a beaker. "New ones are being developed every year. This one is my way of extracting RNA from tissues. Of course, there are others."

"How long can you keep that stuff alive?" Borg asked.

"Refrigerated, a few hours. It has to be applied within twenty-four hours. I usually inject it peritoneally in animals. In humans it would have to be injected intravenously."

Borg did not know what peritoneally meant.

"It looks as though it's going to be a long procedure," Wendtland said. He wanted to go back to the hotel and put a call through to Washington in private. He needed clearance for the financial settlement.

"We'll be working right through the night." Cory measured the liquid brain into small phials, closed them with rubber stoppers, and placed them in a centrifuge, a steel container that looked like a washing machine. He set the time control for fifteen minutes and the speed control at 20,000 rpm. He turned on the current. The needle climbed to 20,000.

Wendtland took off his glasses. "We'd like to stay and watch, but I'm sure we're in your way. Why don't we discuss our private matters tomorrow over lunch at the hotel? By then, I assume, you'll be through with your work"

"Interesting, highly interesting," Wendtland said as they left the laboratory. "Watching him, I had the impression that the experiment might work. He certainly knows what he's doing." He had to get himself in a positive frame of mind before he talked to the gray eminence in the penthouse, a man with a fine ear for people's insecurity.

"What's your impression of Cory?" Slaughter asked.

"Unemotional. Unapproachable. Self-centered. Difficult. Most difficult. I don't think he could ever be bribed. Nor would he do anything out of friendship or human concern, if it didn't fit into the pattern of his work. He's a dangerous man."

"Then he would be especially difficult to handle if he were to get Hauser's memory," Slaughter remarked.

"Yes," Wendtland replied. "I hope you can control him."

Hillel waited until the laboratory door was closed. Then he said: "You could have asked for a hundred thousand, or even half a million. You have them over a barrel, Dottore. And didn't you get the impression that Wendtland wants to put off closing the deal? He doesn't want you to make the experiment until he talks to you again."

His hands were steady as he picked up a slice of brain with forceps and dropped it into a mortar.

"Glad to see that you've adjusted yourself to my sacrifice. What made you change your mind?"

"Your decision. I've known you long enough to interfere only up to a certain point." He picked up a second mortar and carefully measured liquids into it.

"There are so many questions to be answered." Cory plunged the piston down in an empty test tube. "How does the injected material act upon the recipient? I don't mean pathologically.

That we'll find out. The deeper we get involved in these experiments, the more complex they become. Sometimes biochemical approaches raise more questions than they answer. I wonder if the new questions are the right ones."

The telephone rang. Hillel answered it. "For you," he said, passing the receiver to Cory. "It's Queen."

"I want to come over," Queen said without preliminary. "Maybe I can talk you out of this thing."

"What thing?"

"You know what I'm talking about. You mustn't take such a risk. I have an idea I want to discuss with you." He hung up before Cory could reply.

"I wonder who told him," Cory said. "He talks as if I were going to commit suicide. Every important experiment was tried out first by doctors. What's so new about that?"

Hillel did not answer. He picked up a pestle and started grinding the brain in the mortar.

Cory sat down on a high stool. "We'll have to work out a procedure. We'll use the same methods as we did with LSD—tape recorders, questioning, constant observation. However, it's possible that I'll be able to put my sensations down on paper."

"Good," Hillel muttered, "and where will this take place?"

"I've asked Queen to let me have a room at the Medical Center. I arranged with Latour to take over my classes for a time."

"Latour's okay," Hillel muttered almost inaudibly.

"What's the matter with you? You act as if you aren't interested in the experiment anymore. We'll publish the results as a paper for the National Academy of Sciences. Joint authorship. Doesn't that excite you?"

"Of course."

"I'll talk to Karen and tell her you might have to stay with me at the Medical Center for a few days."

"Karen will understand," Hillel said, pouring the contents of the mortar into phials. He passed them to Cory, who placed them in the centrifuge.

What was Hillel being so resentful about? He had worked nights in the lab before.

"In case I'm sick, I've made a scheme of how you should carry on the work. Our next project should be to develop micromethods for studying the chemistry of brain cells and identifying the different RNA factors. I've developed a few ideas on this which I wrote down for you."

"Yes." Hillel looked up from his work as Queen came in quickly and walked straight up to Cory.

"I was at my son's wedding reception. But damn it, I had to talk to you."

"That's quite a sacrifice!" Cory said with a laugh.

"Don't talk about sacrifice." He sat down and watched Cory testing the finely ground matter that had settled at the bottom of a glass tube. The liquids had separated. Cory extracted the fluid containing the RNA with a hypodermic needle and carefully squirted it into a container.

"I've lined up three men from the hospital," Queen said. "Terminal cases. They agree to let us work on them."

"We can't," Cory objected. "You know we can make this experiment only once. We can't go into tests. This is all the RNA we have."

"What's so special about this brain? Why all those people from Washington?"

"Ask them, I don't know."

"And what's the rush? Use my people, all cases with advanced cancer. Anything might help them, who knows. Maybe this is one that works."

Cory bent over the glass that contained Hauser's ribonucleic acids. Silently Hillel opened the centrifuge and inserted the last phials, closed the lid, adjusted the timer and the rpm meter, and switched on the current. The machine hummed.

"Terminal cases would be no good for observation," Cory said. "You know that, Queen. We can't use sick people who have been pumped full of drugs."

Queen turned to Hillel in dismay "Well, do you support Cory's suicidal tendencies?"

"Can you change his mind?"

Wearily Queen got up and polished his glasses. "I reserved two rooms in the psychiatric ward, Cory, as you asked me."

"The psychiatric ward?" Hillel spun around from the centrifuge.

"Sure," Cory said. "Safe from our friends from Washington."

10

Picking up trays and cutlery, Cory, Wendtland, Slaughter, and Borg joined a line of students and slowly moved past the food counter of the university cafeteria.

"Be my guest," Cory said, choosing a plate of salads and asking for a slice of roast beef.

"You're ours, of course," Wendtland said. "After all, we're on an expense account."

His smile was strained. The call to Washington had put him in a quandary. He had been told to conduct the Hauser case at his own discretion. He regretted having come West he should have left the whole affair to Slaughter.

"I'll take you to an expensive restaurant if you insist on picking up the tab," Cory said lightly.

His casualness was a mystery to them all. This man, who was proposing to give himself to a dangerous experiment, showed no signs of apprehension. They expected Cory to be solemn, withdrawn, pensive. His coolness alarmed them.

"What time did you finish last night?" Wendtland asked, as they settled themselves in an island of empty tables.

"About three. We extracted every milligram of RNA."

"When are you going to use it?"

"Tonight. Dr. Queen will be around to observe any pathological changes. I'm going to put a running report of my sensations on tape. Mondoro will be with me constantly."

"What do you mean?" Wendtland was appalled. "Mondoro shouldn't be with you at any time. Look, you don't seem to be fully aware of the importance of the information we might get from you. It certainly mustn't be known to a third party."

"Mondoro isn't a third party," Cory said. "Since I'm conducting the experiment on myself, I'm the sole judge of who will be present and who won't. I've taken rooms in the psychiatric ward. Nobody can get in there without permission. The door's locked."

"But that's impossible!" Borg exclaimed. "That defeats the whole purpose of the idea!"

"Let's assume that the experiment succeeds beyond our expectations. That's possible, isn't it?" Wendtland asked calmly

"Anything is possible."

"All right then. Queen or Mondoro would learn the information from your newly created memory—the dead man's memory. Those secrets must be safeguarded. How do we know your friends won't pass them on—not maliciously, I'm sure, but out of elation, of joy, of pride? What then? That's why we took a man from Sing Sing. He could be handled. Your men can't, legally. That's why I believe that only Mr. Slaughter or somebody else from our office should be with you. We'll supply an expert in your field if you insist, but our man must be there, day and night. Of course, medical help should be on hand— and we can supply that too. But we can't permit an outsider to hear vital secrets."

"I told you that you'll receive a tape with every word said by me or anybody else. But the experiment will be carried out the way I devise it. My objective is strictly scientific. I certainly am not working for the CIA, and I won't permit any interference from you or anybody else."

"Unbelievable," Borg muttered. The man might siphon off important secrets. He might be in touch with the Russians. No idea was too far-fetched. University people had a history of leftist leanings.

"You forget that you don't own that RNA. It's government property."

"Do you legally own that corpse?" Cory grinned, enjoying the fight. "When you turned it over to the Medical Center, you gave it to us for experimentation—what kind of experimentation was left up to us. You can claim the body, though it's slightly damaged. But Queen could restore it to a reasonably good condition."

Slaughter leaned back in his chair, relieved that he was not involved in the argument. Wendtland and Borg were on the spot, not he.

"All right," Wendtland said amicably. "I can see your point. We won't interfere. By the way, Washington agrees on the fee." Wendtland's Junker face cracked into a smile. "I told them that they might get a bargain."

"Good. Send the check to the Dean."

"Dr. Cory?" A young intern in a white coat was approaching the table, flushed and breathless. "Dr. Queen wants you to phone him right away."

Cory got up, visibly alarmed. "Excuse me."

"I wonder what they're up to now," Borg said, watching Cory cross the room.

"Well, since we've got ourselves involved this far, we'll have to go on," said Wendtland. "I had to give in to Cory. I told you it's no use fighting him. You only make him more stubborn. We'll put a continuous tail on him. Twenty-four hours, reporting every three hours. Also on Mondoro and Queen. And their families. Record their calls. Run a complete dossier check on them. You'll look after that, Slaughter."

"I'll make the necessary local contacts immediately." Slaughter was in his element again.

The three men watched Cory threading his way back through the tables. His face was gray. His eyes seemed to have sunk deeper into their sockets.

"You'll excuse me," he said hurriedly. "I must go over to the psychiatric ward."

"Anything wrong?" Wendtland asked.

"I should've guessed as much," Cory said in distress. "What a fool I was!"

"What's the matter, Dr. Cory," asked Borg. "Has something

happened?"

"It certainly has" said Cory grimly. "Dr. Mondoro has injected the RNA into himself."

11

It was not the first time Karen had picked up Hillel at the hospital; he often worked there. Every afternoon at four he phoned and told her where to meet him. But this time—and for the first time—Cory had telephoned. So it was with a sigh of relief that she saw Hillel and Cory leave the hospital together. Cory's hand was under Hillel's elbow—only when they came close did she see her husband's deadly pallor. Quickly she pushed the door open and Cory shoved Hillel inside.

Karen touched her husband's cheek. "You're sick."

"Not very," Cory assured her, but he said no more. It frightened her.

Queen had objected to Hillel's leaving the ward, but Cory, an M.D. himself, felt it advisable to let Hillel go home. Not only was he physically able to do so, but it would keep him away from the prying curiosity of the CIA men.

Karen drove slowly, listening to Hillel's labored breathing. "What's the matter with him?" she asked Cory, bulldozing her way through the rush-hour traffic into a side street. Neither answered and her anxiety increased.

"I swallowed the wrong medicine," Hillel finally said jokingly. He coughed and his face contorted.

Karen accelerated. She knew Cory would have made him stay at the hospital if he had been seriously ill, but the strange silence between the two men upset her more and more.

She drove the car jerkily into the garage of their apartment house. Cory helped Hillel out. In the yellow neon of the elevator, Hillel looked older. Fine creases ran from the corner of his eyes to the temples and from mouth to chin. For a moment he looked like his father. And moved like him, stooped, his left shoulder lifted.

"He'll be all right by tomorrow," Cory muttered uncomfortably as they entered the apartment. "Why don't you go to bed and sleep, Hillel?"

Wordlessly he shuffled off, and Karen followed him. Cory took a small tape recorder from his pocket. Knowing how close Hillel and Karen were, he felt sure Hillel would tell her about the injection eventually. But it was essential he gain her confidence at once. He needed her help.

Cory realized with surprise he was proceeding on the supposition that the experiment would succeed.

"Why are you sitting in the dark?" Karen had come in so quietly she startled him. Night had fallen; the room was bathed in shadows.

"No special reason. Sit down."

Her eyes shone luminously, the rest of her features dissolved in semidarkness. "Won't you tell me what happened?"

"Hillel will."

"I tried to talk to him, but he fell asleep."

"He's going to tell you right now," Cory said, and turned on the tape recorder. Hillel's voice emerged:

"In case I become incapacitated, I'm putting down the following information for Dr. Cory. I am injecting the RNA into myself because Dr. Cory has decided to volunteer for the test. Being younger than he, I am in better physical condition, and it is inconceivable that Dr. Cory's work should be endangered. I have decided to inject the full amount of the extracted RNA. The amount is exactly twelve hundred thirty-five milligrams. I have dissolved it in five cc of saline solution and now I shall administer the shot intravenously into my left arm."

For a few seconds the voice stopped. The sound of steel touching glass came from the recorder. Then Hillel's voice returned, matter-of-factly, but with increasing tension.

"The sensation is an extensive burning, and I can trace the solution's progress through my veins into the cavity of my chest muscles. Spasms in the diaphragm start."

Heavy, labored breathing, and then the sound of a telephone dial came from the loudspeaker.

"Dr. Queen's office?" Hillel's voice broke. "This is Mondoro at ten-o-four. Tell Dr. Queen to come over right away—emergency!" A gasp. The sound of the telephone receiver hitting the table. "Cramps. Spasms. My stomach's on fire. Mouth seems to be filled with acid. Vision blurred. I think I'm ... going to pass out...." No more words; only moans. Cory turned off the switch.

"Horrible," Karen said in a dead voice.

"I'd better turn on the light."

Karen's face, always ivory pale, had gone dead white. Her lips, painted stark red, looked like blood.

"There's more on the tape, but this is what I wanted you to know," Cory said levelly. "I'm sure Hillel wouldn't have told it this way."

"No. If he told me at all. He never mentions unhappiness or fears to me. But what's going to happen now?"

"Possibly nothing," Cory said. "He's over the shock now and may have no aftereffects, although RNA ordinarily is given in small doses over an extended period of time. I had no idea he meant to substitute himself for me. If I had, I would have interfered."

"I know you would," Karen said. "He was afraid you might stop him. He talks about you as if he expects you to solve all the world's ills. If I had known that you wanted to go through this test, I'd have guessed what Hillel would do. But what is this stuff he has taken?"

"Hillel will tell you when he's had some rest. But just now we have to make sure he gets better quickly." Cory leaned forward. "I need your help, Karen. We must take all precautions possible, since I can't anticipate what kind of effect this injection will have. I want you to report to me every single change you see in him. In health or behavior."

"Change? You think there'll be a change in him?"

"Now, now, there's no need to get alarmed," he said. "I don't expect any aftereffects, and if there are any, Hillel will tell me. But if by chance something does escape him, please let me know at once."

"I'm terrified."

"There's no reason to be. It's only natural that he will experience some sensations, because his brain has been stimulated. Many drugs, mescaline and LSD for instance, produce pathological reactions of one kind or another. Our imagination responds to all of them. But the aftereffects disappear in a short time."

"My mother warned me not to marry a scientist," she said, confidence returning to her voice. "She said I should marry a shoe clerk, who leaves his troubles behind when he comes home from work. He wouldn't think of shoes, he'd think only of me."

"Doesn't Hillel?"

She nodded then suddenly stiffened. A moment later Cory heard Hillel's scream. She ran into the bedroom.

Hillel was propped up in bed, his eyes closed, his face distorted with fear. Again he screamed.

"Hillel! Hillel!" Karen shook him violently.

He opened his eyes wide and stared at her. "What happened?"

"You screamed," she said, still shocked.

"Did I?" He slid deeper into the bed. "I didn't know. It must have been a nightmare."

He turned to Cory, his voice sober and controlled. "It was like a nightmare drugs produce—reserpine, amytal, phenobarbital. It was vivid." The color was coming back into his face, but the look of horror was still in his eyes.

"A nightmare?" Cory pulled a chair close to the bed. "Do you remember it?"

"He never dreams," Karen said.

Hillel's long fingers were shaking on the bedsheet. Karen picked up his hand, covering it with both of hers.

"Let me record my dream on tape, Dottore. It might be related to the RNA."

"Why don't you keep quiet," Karen pleaded. "Please, Dottore, tell him not to excite himself."

Hillel threw back the bedcovers. "I didn't inject that stuff to be treated like a sick man," he said. "Let me record the dream as long as it's fresh in my mind."

"I'll remember it for you. You'd better stay here," Cory said. Karen gently covered him with the bedclothes.

"A bombing," Hillel said, and collapsed on his pillow.

"A war?" Cory asked.

"Yes, I heard air-raid sirens, and then came the bombs. First from afar, then closer and closer. They whistled before they hit. There was no place to run or hide."

"You haven't been in a war," Cory said in a neutral voice. "How did you know it was a bombing? From movies, TV?"

Hillel closed his eyes; his face was strained. "I was in a shelter with a lot of people. Some were in uniform." He suddenly laughed, surprised and incredulous. "Nazi uniforms."

"Have you seen a Nazi picture lately, or read a book about them?"

"I have," Karen said. "It's still here next to my bed." She picked up the book; on its cover was a blood-red swastika.

"That's what might have triggered your dream," Cory said.

"I can't remember seeing the book, but how can I be sure?" Hillel said. "I'm absentminded, and I only see what I want to see."

"Try to recall the surroundings of your dream or familiar faces," Cory pressed him gently.

"I didn't know anybody, though the people were strangely familiar to me. But I knew it was I in the shelter. I wore a uniform."

"Are you sure?" Cory asked, trying to be objective and not connect this to the German whose RNA he had extracted.

"No—I can't say for sure. I watched myself in that dream, and in a detached way, too. It was so vivid that I wasn't sure if I was awake or dreaming. I remember I wore a gold ring with a crest made of a gold deer's head on a blue stone; it was heavy, maybe a fraternity ring." Hillel looked at his hand. "I can even feel where it made an imprint." He lifted his hand close to his eyes.

"It was a dream, remember," Karen said urgently.

"But why can I still feel the imprint?" Hillel turned to Cory for an answer. "Sometimes one only remembers parts of dreams. I might have dreamed much more and forgotten."

"What else do you remember?" Cory suppressed his eagerness to question Hillel too severely. It was too early to force him to evaluate his nightmare; he was a sick man.

"Every time a bomb hit nearby, things fell down," Hillel said vaguely.

"What kind of things?"

"Instruments slid off tables. Electronic equipment. Radios, vacuum tubes, the kind they used in the thirties, not transistorized. There were inscriptions in German on boxes and on the wall."

"You don't speak German, remember?" Cory had to be cautious, subject evidence to the most stringent tests; dreams have their own logic, a logic that has nothing to do with the logic of scientific research.

"No, I don't, although I know Yiddish. But these were words I had never seen before. Strange, but I still see them now: *Notausgang, Hauptschaltunge hochspannung.*"

"What makes you sure you've never heard or read them?" Cory pressed on. "You've looked at books written in German we have a lot in the library. They might have lingered in your subconscious and appeared in your dream.

Exhausted, Hillel closed his eyes. "That attack took the stuffing out of me," he muttered, and instantly fell asleep.

Karen took his lifeless hand. Misery was written in every line of her body, in the bend of her slim back, in the dark hair falling around her thin shoulders. She sat quietly, watching Hillel's waxen face.

Cory nodded to her. Slowly she withdrew her hand from Hillel's and followed Cory out of the bedroom.

"Do you think it was simply a dream?" she whispered. "Something his mind has made up? Or could it be"—she looked at him in fright—"someone else's memory?"

12

"He's in good shape," Queen said, returning the blood pressure gauge to its case. "One hundred twenty-five over eighty-five. The diastole was a little high yesterday, but not today. Reflexes normal."

"Headaches?" Cory asked Hillel.

"No. Some more dreams, but not as vivid as the first. Of landscapes I've never seen, and modern industrial plants. Atom reactors. A river. A little house. All unknown to me. But I'm suspicious of my own observations. Every sensation I attribute to the effects of the RNA, and it might be all imagination. I'm watching my cravings and desires and wishes as if they were abnormal, though some I have always had and have never paid attention to. But what's new to me are these depressions. I've never had those. And they're followed by images. I'm writing everything down and I'll let you be the judge, Dottore."

"All these sensations could be aftereffects of the drug."

"Don't you think you should talk to Slaughter?" Queen asked.

"He calls me at least twice a day."

"There's nothing definite to report," Cory said. "The first reaction has been violent. That was to be expected."

"If we knew more about that donor!" Queen said. "Slaughter and Wendtland must know his history. They could make comparisons between the man's background and Mondoro's dreams."

"That makes sense," Hillel said eagerly. "If only I knew who that man was."

"We have no facts for any comparison," Cory said patiently.

"We might never have," Hillel said. "But if Slaughter were to compare my sensory impressions with the dead man's life—like my dream of the bombing—that would be a start. The German uniforms I saw and can still describe minutely belong to World War II. The kind of instruments I saw are out of date. What does that mean?"

"You told us he was a German," Queen said.

"Yes. Slaughter said he was."

"And I deduced that he was in World War II," Hillel said. "I've read enough about that time to have nightmares even without the man's RNA!"

Hillel's attempted cheerfulness fooled no one. He worried about the strange. new thoughts that came into his mind; about the mental pictures of streets where he had never been; vivid landscapes; a tree standing against a cloudy sky with corpses hanging from its limbs. He analyzed every one of his emotions and desires, even his appetite, as though his taste buds were controlled not by him but by some demon that had invaded his body. He turned to Karen even more than before; at night she slept in his arms, as though listening to his dreams, ready to wake him if a nightmare attacked. Never had he felt so close to her as now.

"Slaughter calls me ten times a day," Cory said. "He has become a nuisance. I tell him exactly what you report to me: the experiment hasn't produced any tangible results."

"He's afraid the foreign RNA will lose its potency—if there's such a thing as memory transfer at all. He wants information right now and doesn't trust us. I can't blame him," Hillel said, with an attempt at a smile. "But there's nothing to report, Dottore."

"Nothing?" Cory asked casually.

He was aware of an evasiveness, as if Hillel resented his prying into secrets too personal to reveal.

"I would tell you, wouldn't I?" Hillel said.

"Of course you would."

Cory knew Hillel was not speaking the truth—Karen had called and asked him to see her.

They met in an ice cream parlor on Santa Monica Boulevard, the only adults among the noisy teen-agers from a nearby high school.

"I feel like we're conspirators," she whispered, reaching out to touch Cory's sleeve. "This is one place Hillel won't look for us. He hates ice cream."

"I've put him on an assignment that should keep him busy for several hours," Cory said. "Can I get you a cup of coffee?"

She nodded. When he returned with two cups of coffee, she was making up her lips. Looking intently into the mirror, she did not raise her eyes.

"How's my spy doing?"

"Badly," she said, snapping the compact closed. "Maybe it's only in my mind, but I see changes in Hillel. Tell me that I'm only imagining things."

"What things?"

"Since Hillel recovered from that shock, he has become less—how shall I say—less honest."

Cory seemed surprised at her choice of words. "What has he done that's dishonest?"

"Not exactly dishonest," she said. "But I have the feeling that he's acting a part. He *tries* to be the Hillel I know. He's consciously adhering to the character he believes he was before."

Cory watched her quietly.

"He forces himself to be relaxed in my presence," she continued. "There's something going on in his mind that I can only feel—I can't put it into words."

"You have to tell me concrete facts, or I can't understand you," Cory said.

"It's very personal," she said. "At night I sometimes have the feeling that he doubts himself...."

"Doubts himself?"

"Yes, he will sometimes move away from me suddenly, as though afraid of being in the same bed with me."

"Perhaps he senses you're acting strangely and he's reacting to you—isn't that possible?"

She thought this over and shook her head.

"I love him more than ever. But sometimes I feel he isn't Hillel—that he's somebody else."

"He's off balance, and so are you," Cory said. "You're still experiencing the shock you felt when he came home from the hospital. Now he's not behaving exactly as he used to and as you expect him to, you imagine that something's wrong. Nothing is. Your fears are part of your deep love for Hillel. Now he really needs you and shows it, and that frightens you—you're afraid you may be unequal to his heightened demands."

"Are you sure?" Her eyes seemed to light up with hope.

"Sure? In my profession one never really is sure of anything. Of course, I want to believe that the experiment is showing results. But I can't let my wishes becloud my observations. So far, I must assume that there's no real proof. Act like a scientist, Karen. Don't let yourself be upset by conjecture."

"This isn't conjecture," she said soberly. "He has a new interest that occupies him all the time. Electromagnetism. Has he told you about it?"

"No."

"He brings home books about magnetism, piles of them, and reads them like novels. And German history. In German! But he doesn't know German."

Cory tried not to show his surprise.

"There's nothing strange about an interest in electromagnetism. As for German, he does know Yiddish, after all."

She seemed unconvinced. "It's as if Hillel has become two people—himself and the *dybbuk.*"

"*Dybbuk?*"

"A devil that takes over a soul. The Jews believe in it." She laughed. "It sounds silly, doesn't it?" Suddenly she started to cry.

The teen-agers at the next table eyed her and stopped talking.

"Karen," Cory said, "I don't believe in ghosts, Jewish or otherwise."

She made an effort to control herself, and sipped her coffee.

"I'm being silly."

"You wouldn't have these ideas if you didn't know about the RNA experiment."

"I would have. I love him too much not to know."

Cory was worried by Karen's report. Now he was sure that Hillel was holding back information. But why? He would have expected that attitude from Foster, the convict, or from the dead scientist. A defector who had been a German national sent to a concentration camp would be trained in subterfuge.

But not Hillel. Was his unusual behavior an outcome of the RNA experiment? It was possible that foreign RNA in the cortex produced changes in character. Cory had observed rats, after having been given the RNA of a hamster enter the treadmills of hamsters. But Karen's report had to be verified by Hillel before he could arrive at any conclusion.

He found Hillel still working at the lab. He offered to walk him home.

Hillel hung up his coat, gathered a book, and set off with Cory. The tension between them was tangible.

"I wonder if you're still interested in the RNA experiment," Cory said, after some moments of silence.

"Why that question?"

"You know why. We started out as collaborators."

"We still are."

"Then why are you holding back information from me?"

"I'm not aware that I am."

"You never tell me about your observations voluntarily. I have to extract them from you like pulling teeth. You've certainly changed your attitude toward the experiment—and toward me."

Hillel did not reply.

"You almost killed yourself in your eagerness to keep me out of danger. But now you're keeping the results to yourself. I must know why."

"I don't know," Hillel said, turning to him. "I really don't. I want to talk to you, but I can't. I would feel guilty if I talked to you."

"Guilty?"

"Yes. As if I were … betraying myself—and some cause that I can't define. Of course, I analyze my feelings, Dottore. I realize that my interest in my work has diminished to a point where I have to force myself to continue. Instead I find myself fascinated by a new problem that has nothing to do with chemistry or biochemistry."

Hillel looked probingly at Cory, as if for an explanation.

"This is a pertinent change in you," Cory said. "Why did you keep it to yourself?"

"Well—because it disturbs me," Hillel said unhappily. "You tell me why I want to read this."

He held out the book he was carrying.

"Die Revolution des Nihilismus," Cory read aloud.

"In German. I never studied German."

"But you can read it?"

"At first I could only pick out words, but after a few days I had no trouble reading them all. Most books I take home are in German."

"Do you use a dictionary?"

"I haven't got one."

"But you understand Yiddish."

"It doesn't help with words like *Ersatzmittelwirtschaft* and *Bevolkerungsdruck*. They don't exist in Yiddish."

"Do you think that proves that learning can be transferred chemically?"

"It certainly is a phenomenon," Hillel said. "But I wouldn't dare arrive at a conclusion on this evidence alone."

"The RNA came from a man who spoke German. It was his native language."

"Yes. And it's not the only engram I've observed. It doesn't stop with memory transfer. I'm suffering from sudden attacks of depression which terrify me. They seem to precede memory recall, as if the depressions were the trigger of the recall." He stopped, and Cory sensed the struggle going on in Hillel's mind.

"Memory recall?" Cory said questioningly.

But Hillel ignored the question and went on, "I take refuge in Karen's strength at those moments. Because I feel absolutely lost. Of course, she's aware I'm distressed, and she's frightened."

"Have you talked all this over with her?"

"No. What could I tell her? No wonder I'm all mixed up. There are moments, Dottore, when I look at Karen as if she were a stranger. I come into my apartment and don't know why I'm there, and sometimes you too seem to be an outsider I mustn't trust. A tremendous impatience surges up in me at those moments. and I know I

shouldn't be at the campus, or talking to you, or with Karen. I should be somewhere else."

"Where?" Cory tried to mask his concern.

"If I only knew, I'd know the answer to everything that's torturing me!"

Neither of them spoke until they had reached Hillel's apartment house. But Hillel made no move to enter.

"What's happening to me, Dottore?"

"The RNA has upset you mentally. That seems evident, the only evidence I accept as proven. You're digging yourself deeper into a depression that may have no pathological origin. Let's look at the facts rationally," Cory said. "We've established that memory can be transferred chemically in animals. You might have proved that it's also possible in humans.

Though this needs confirmation, and it can only be done by using other people, under the same conditions. Podgorsky wrote about memory transfer in hamsters and rats, and there are Heller's and countless other biochemists' experiments. What you're experiencing isn't conclusive proof. We have to take into consideration that the powerful shot you gave yourself upset you. It should have been done gradually, which would have given us a chance of precise observation. Being high-strung, you jump to the conclusion that these emotions you're feeling are character changes. But they're more like a pregnant woman's craving for blueberries in winter. They are whims. They have no basis in scientific fact. They'll pass."

"So I'm pregnant," Hillel said with a smile; "That would be earthshaking! Maybe you're right. In any case, I feel better already. Wait till I tell Karen. I know it will make her happy." He started inside. "Will you join us for dinner, Dottore?"

Cory declined. Let Karen enjoy her husband's good mood all by herself. He hailed a passing cab and waved at Hillel, still at the entrance.

Later he wondered if events would have turned out differently if he had gone upstairs and never let Hillel from his sight.

Cory ate alone. He liked the anonymity of sitting in a restaurant unrecognized, walking for hours along streets he did not know. After dinner in a colorless restaurant on Pico Boulevard, he walked through sleepy little streets, past Spanish houses, drifting aimlessly while his mind worked with its usual rigid precision.

But he could not shake off a feeling of uneasiness, and he stopped at a telephone booth and called Hillel's apartment. It was eleven o'clock at night. Karen answered so quickly she must have had her hand on the receiver.

"Where's Hillel?" she cried.

"What do you mean'?" Cory asked. "I left him hours ago at

the entrance to your building."

"Where is he?"

He could feel the fear in her.

"I'll be over at your place in a few minutes."

"Yes, come soon," Karen cried. Her voice broke.

It took Cory a long time to get a taxi. When he arrived at Hillel's apartment, Karen was standing in the open door.

"What could've happened to him?" she asked, as if Cory knew the answer.

"I don't know."

"He's always on time' or he calls me," she said. Her control was a thin veneer which might crack at any moment.

"Let's check the hospitals and the police stations."

"I've already done that. They haven't anybody by that name, and I know Hillel carries credit cards with his name and address. I talked to the police station downtown. The man told me to wait till tomorrow morning. He'd call me if he had any news. He said almost all missing persons turn up, and asked me if Hillel drank or if he'd ever stayed out all night before. And if we'd had a quarrel."

"All we can do is wait," Cory said, sitting down. "He might have a good reason for not coming upstairs. Maybe he went back to the lab. Did you call the night watchman at the campus?"

"That was the first thing I did."

The doorbell cut into her voice.

"There he is," she cried, running to the door. Cory heard a familiar voice. Slaughter's.

"I'm sorry I couldn't get over here sooner, Mrs. Mondoro. I was trying to raise Washington and Dr. Cory, and then your phone was busy. I could have saved you much distress," he said with the calmness of a man used to excitement.

"You know where Hillel is?" Karen asked eagerly.

Slaughter's coolness made her a degree less anxious. Hillel

must be alive and well or Slaughter would not have been so calm. Slaughter did not answer her question. He turned to Cory.

"I had hoped to meet you here."

"Please come to the point," Cory said. "Where is Dr. Mondoro?"

"By now," Slaughter said, looking at his watch, "he should be flying over the North Pole."

Karen looked at him aghast.

"You can't be serious," Cory said.

"Oh, but I am." Slaughter put down his hat carefully on a small table. "Dr. Mondoro took the seven ten SAS plane out of International Airport. If he had taken Pan Am or TWA, he would've flown to Europe via New York and we would've had a chance to dissuade him."

"Europe?" Karen sat down shakily.

"He bought a ticket to Frankfurt and Prague. One-way ticket. Of course, he'll have to change planes in Copenhagen."

Karen covered her mouth with both hands.

"But I left him downstairs at six," Cory said.

Slaughter took out a thin notebook. "You took a taxi at six-o-three. Mondoro waited downstairs for seven minutes, and then at six ten stopped a taxi, drove to the airport, arrived at six fifty-eight, and boarded the plane at seven ten."

"But why ..." Karen's voice trailed off dazedly.

"Dr. Cory might know," Slaughter said expectantly.

"I don't know, and it doesn't make sense," Cory said, but he was remembering Hillel's outburst: I *should be somewhere else.*

"Dottore," Karen said helplessly, the one person now she could turn to for protection.

"We have had Dr. Mondoro under constant surveillance. of course. since you refused to cooperate with us," Slaughter said severely. "He had a passport on him, or he wouldn't have been able to travel. It was issued two years ago in Los Angeles be-fore he attended a symposium in Stockholm. I suspect that he kept the document in his office. He had no money on him and cashed a check on his American Express credit card. He bought the ticket with that card. No luggage. At the airport he bought a flight bag and some toilet articles for the trip, two pairs of socks, and a washable shirt."

He turned his body stiffly to face Karen. "Whom does he know in Europe?"

Karen put her hand on Cory's arm for support.

"Nobody I know of," she said. "We met some people in Stockholm two years ago. But I don't think he ever corresponded with them."

"Did he give you any indication that he wanted to leave the country?"

"No."

"Nor to you, Dr. Cory?"

"He mentioned tonight that he should be somewhere else," Cory said. "But he didn't tell me where he wanted to be."

Slaughter made a note.

"Could it be that his sudden departure has something to do with the experiment?"

"Possibly."

"Did he appear normal to you after the experiment?" Slaughter looked probingly first at Karen and then at Cory.

"I couldn't say for sure," Cory said. "All I can offer is conjecture, and that has no value."

"I don't know what proof a scientist needs in order to make a positive statement," Slaughter said disgustedly. "I know that you can't put conjectures into test tubes or computers. But you were together every day. Nothing extraordinary aroused your suspicions?"

"The memory transfer worked the way it worked in test animals—that is to say, there are indications that it did. I wouldn't presume to state that his emotional change is the result of the RNA injection."

Slaughter's face reddened. "As a lawyer I know how to be evasive." His voice rose angrily. "But you scientists obfuscate the issue till it disappears. Let me give you the facts without laboratory tests. Mondoro transferred Hauser's memory to himself. That's the dead man's name, Karl Hellmuth Hauser. No point in keeping it a secret any longer. We had a deal with you. We were to be informed by you or Mondoro about every step of this experiment, every bit of progress. We paid for that service. You deliberately kept us in the dark, heaven only knows why. Now Mondoro has run away to Europe. I couldn't hold him back. He's a private citizen and can do whatever he wants. His going was no criminal act. But now we're at an impasse for which I can blame only you."

Slaughter let the accusation hang in the air. He had no intention of telling them that right at this moment one of his men was on the plane with Hillel Mondoro.

13

Hillel felt a soft hand on his shoulder and opened his eyes. Hazily, as through a veil, he saw a stewardess bending over him.

"Sorry to wake you, sir," the face above him said, "but we're landing in Reykjavik in a few minutes. Please fasten your seat belt."

"Reykjavik," Hillel muttered. His head hurt as if encircled by an iron band.

"Iceland. Only for refueling."

Hillel looked around him. He was close to panic. What was he doing in a plane? How did he get there? Where was he going? An endless gray cloud covered the world below. Mechanically he snapped the seat belt shut, then searched his pockets for the flight ticket.

Los Angeles, Copenhagen, Frankfurt, Prague ...

The ticket was issued in his name. It had been tucked into his passport. Another name was on the tip of his tongue, a name as well known to him as his own but which he could not recall. Maybe if he could remember the name, he would know why he was flying to Copenhagen. To Frankfurt. To Prague. He went through the alphabet, trying to connect every letter with that elusive name. It did not work.

Hillel closed his eyes. The foreign RNA in him had blotted out his consciousness, paralyzed his free will. Would it continue to direct him? If he lost control over himself the whole experiment would become futile. He had to phone Karen as soon as he could get to a telephone—and Cory. Cory wouldn't have been panicked by the situation. He would have observed his condition with detachment, perhaps with curiosity. There was no immediate emergency—after all, he was sitting well protected in a comfortable DC-8. Now he had the proof that he and Cory wanted: the RNA *was* influencing consciousness, and his observations had not been figments of his imagination.

Hillel looked out of the window again. The clouds broke jaggedly and revealed a coastline and small ships below, and then land covered with ice and snow. Air pressure increased in his eardrums and aggravated his headache as the plane descended, hitting the runway with a soft thud.

"Amazing," Hillel said aloud. He felt better for having sized up the situation.

"That's the first time I've heard you speak," said the man beside him. "You worried me. You've slept continuously since you boarded the plane."

Hillel smiled; he did not want to be drawn into a conversation.

"The stewardess wanted to wake you up when meals were served, but I told her to let you sleep. I thought you might need sleep more than food."

The man had a round, childlike face and a good-natured expression.

The plane came to a stop; snowdrifts surrounded the airport.

"Will all passengers please leave the plane," the stewardess' voice came from the loudspeaker. "Please board the bus waiting outside. The flight will continue in approximately half an hour."

She repeated the instructions in three more languages.

"It's ten below outside," the man beside Hillel said. "Don't you have an overcoat?"

Hillel shook his head and walked along the aisle and down the steep ladder. The cold air stabbed his lungs and stopped his breath for a moment. His cheeks contracted from the impact of the needle-sharp wind, but the panic had left him.

A bus took the passengers to an overheated hut. A small stand sold dolls dressed like Eskimos, colorful blankets, and loud hand-knitted sweaters. Coffee was being served in a corner. A postal clerk pushed open a window marked "Post Office."

Hillel looked through his pockets, found his small notebook of addresses and a folder of traveler's checks. How did he get the checks? They had his signature.

"Can I reach Los Angeles by phone?" Hillel asked the clerk.

"Now?" said the man in surprise. "It might take hours."

"Can't you speed it up?"

"I could get you through on 'Blitz,' and you'd have it at once. But that'd cost you three times the ordinary rate."

"That's all right," Hillel said, and gave a number in Brentwood, California.

Cory would understand and advise. He would call Karen, who must be near distraction by now, and console her.

"There's a booth at the end of the restaurant," the man behind the counter said. "Just pick up the receiver when you hear the ring."

Hillel went to the washroom and bent close to the mirror. His face was grayish white. Lines encircled his mouth, deep crevices cut into his cheeks, wrinkles had dug themselves around his eyes, which looked fatigued.

"You must have left Los Angeles in a hurry. You don't even carry a toothbrush. I can't travel without my slippers." The small man with the round face stood behind Hillel. He held out a calling card.

"Krensky," the man said, when Hillel made no move to take it, pocketed the card without showing offense. "IBM—International Business Machines—Frankfurt."

"Hauser," Hillel said aloud. "Karl Hellmuth Hauser." The name simply came to his lips.

For a moment the man looked startled, then his childlike face reverted to its usual good humor.

"Glad to meet you, Mr. Hauser. Are you going to Copenhagen for the first time? I know it well."

Hillel shook his head and left. As he closed the door to the washroom he heard the telephone ring urgently.

Cory looked at the clock as the telephone rang. It was five in the morning. Only a couple of hours ago he had returned from Karen's apartment. He had talked very little; she sat close to the telephone, as if Hillel were going to call any moment. She was not afraid; she was convinced that Hillel would turn up.

Finally Cory had left and taken a walk. He could think better when he was alone. Hillel had acted independently, a possibility he had not taken into consideration—though Hillel's behavior during the past few days should have prepared him. Had Hillel lost control over his actions? And how much was Hauser's RNA influencing Hillel's behavior?

"A call for Dr. Cory. Hold the line."

"It's Hillel."

"Where are you?"

"In Reykjavik, on my way to Copenhagen, and it's damn cold." Hillel's voice sounded controlled. "It seems that the effects of the RNA are accumulating. I don't even know how I got on the plane."

"You drove straight to the airport, bought a ticket at the SAS counter with your credit card, and bought three hundred dollars' worth of traveler's checks."

"Did Slaughter tell you? If he watched me, why didn't he stop me?"

"He couldn't legally. And I don't think he wanted to. Why, I don't know."

"Now we have proof that the injection worked!" Hillel said excitedly. "I even remember the name of the man— Karl Hellmuth Hauser Is that correct?"

"Yes," Cory said. "Who told you?"

"Nobody," Hillel said. "The name popped up in my memory. Or should I say his memory? What do you suggest I should do?

Take the next plane home?"

"What do you want to do?"

"I—I must go on to Copenhagen," Hillel said.

"Why?"

"If I only knew. But I can't shake the idea that I must go there. It's like a compulsion. I feel it's what I've wanted to do for years. Visit Copenhagen. Not the city, but somebody who lives there."

"Who?" Cory's personal feelings for Hillel were superseded by his scientific curiosity.

"I don't know," Hillel said. "But I have to go. These thoughts are preceded by mental depressions that I can't control."

"Then go on," Cory said, "don't fight the compulsion. I'd rather know where you'll be and join you than lose you again. I know Copenhagen. Take a couple of rooms at the Hotel Europa. I'll be there on the next plane."

"The Europa," Hillel repeated, and Cory had the impression that he was relieved not to be told to return home.

"I'll talk to Karen and tell her that you're all right."

"Do that."

Cory heard the blurred voice on the loudspeaker announcing the continuation of the flight.

"We started an experiment and we have to see it through," Hillel said. "I know I can handle that other— person in me. Anyhow, we're a team, Dottore."

Cory knew that Hillel needed assurance, that his apparent calm was a brittle shell. "Just wait in Copenhagen at the hotel. Leave the rest to me," he said.

It was not Hillel Mondoro he was speaking to, it was a human guinea pig. There was no room for sentiment or friendship or personal considerations. Only one objective was important—the empirical test of RNA transfer. Nothing else mattered to Cory. Or, it seemed, to Hillel either.

"The RNA will gradually lose its power, so we must observe

it as long as it's active in you."

"It's frightening," Hillel said, and for the first time Cory realized just how terrified he was. "I wish you were here."

"In a few hours ..." Cory said. "I guess I would've been frightened too, if I'd been the recipient. But it's frightening only as long as we are dealing with unknown factors. If we can analyze them successfully, the fear will disappear."

"I guess you're right," Hillel said. "I'm sure it would be better not to tell Karen where I am. She can be very stubborn, and I don't want her to chase after me. Tell her we'll be back in a day or so."

"I will."

"Now they're calling my name for the departure. I'll see you in Copenhagen."

"Yes, and stay at the hotel!"

Cory had just put down the receiver when the telephone rang.

"Why did you encourage Mondoro to travel on when we need him here?" Slaughter's voice was calm and unhurried.

"I forgot that you tap phones," Cory said drily. "But I thought it would be safer if I joined him. He might get lost on the way home."

"He won't get lost," Slaughter said. "I have him watched. Maybe you should meet him in Copenhagen. You might find out why he went there. It seems that stuff is taking effect. Washington will flip when I tell them."

"Don't!" Cory said sharply. "Wait. There's nothing yet to report that can help you. You might upset the whole experiment. Keep out of it."

"Yes, boss," Slaughter said sarcastically. "And now, take a piece of advice from me for a change. Don't talk to his wife. Let me tell her that she's going to have her hubby back in forty-eight hours."

"You're very helpful," Cory said derisively.

"Don't ever forget that it might've been you we're chasing instead of this guy. I wish Mondoro hadn't interfered. He doesn't seem to have your mental stability. He's prone to depressions."

"He wasn't before," Cory said. "And they must be severe, or he wouldn't complain."

"My assistant just gave me a note. Your plane will leave in forty-five minutes. TWA direct. There will be a car at your door in five minutes. I'll see you on the plane. I love Copenhagen."

"You stay out of this," Cory said. "Slaughter, if you go on interfering, I promise you, you'll lose both of us. It's my experiment and Mondoro's, not yours."

"That's debatable," Slaughter said. "I didn't expect you to get emotional too. But don't kid yourself: we'll stay on his tail—and yours. What you need is protection. And we'll see to it that you don't run out on us with Hauser's memory!"

14

Walking down Andersens Boulevard in Copenhagen after having checked into the hotel where he had taken two rooms, one for himself and an adjoining one for Cory, Hillel could not shake the feeling that he was walking beside another person, and that other person knew Copenhagen well—a city Hillel had never visited.

A church steeple of verdigrised copper rose from a square base of bricks; verdigrised cupolas covered stately buildings; cars were parked in endless rows—Volvos, Renaults, Austins—diminutive automobiles, accented by a few American behemoths. Traffic lights flashed, but neither the pedestrians nor the moving cars seemed to take any notice of them. Hillel was directed from within to cross the street. A tiny car racing by almost touched him without slowing down. Narrow-chested, brick-built houses stood leaning against each other like toys; shops descended below the street level; the sidewalks were narrow and paved with flat stones.

A sign reading *"Privatebanken,"* the lettering curving around the god Mercury speeding on winged feet, caught Hillel's eye. He went into the bank and presented his traveler's checks.

"May I have your passport, please?" the teller asked. "And please sign the checks down here in the right-hand corner."

"Karl Hellmuth Hauser," Hillel said. The name forced itself to his lips.

"Hauser?" the teller looked up from the passport quickly. "Here it says Dr. Hillel Mondoro."

"Yes, Mondoro, that's my name." He was Hillel Mondoro, not Karl Hauser; but Hauser was the name engraved in his mind.

"Sign here, please." The teller passed a pen to Hillel and watched the slender young American in the unseasonable summer suit suspiciously as he hesitated and glanced at the signature on the check.

"Hillel Mondoro," he wrote in precise handwriting. The teller looked at the signature, comparing it with the name Hillel had written on the checks in Los Angeles.

"This isn't the same handwriting," the teller said sharply.

"Of course it is—I bought those checks myself and signed them."

"You've signed with a European script. Quite different from that on the check."

"Did I?" Hillel asked curiously. He felt wrapped in a cocoon and looked at the world around him dispassionately. The feeling of unreality had not left him since he had started to follow his alter ego, his *Doppelgänger*. But he felt safe, detached from the world.

"One moment, please," the teller said, and disappeared, taking the passport and the checks with him, returning with a meticulously dressed man with a monocle in his right eye.

"Lindtquist," the man introduced himself. "I'm the manager. You're Dr. Mondoro?"

"Yes."

"I suggest you go to American Express to cash the checks. It's in the Dagmarhus on Andersens Boulevard, not far from here."

"But why can't you cash them?" Hillel asked.

"I'm sorry, but American Express is the right place." Lindtquist turned to leave.

"The checks are all right. I can vouch for them," a voice said, and Hillel discovered Krensky standing beside him, his round face creased in a pleasant smile. "Here is my passport. I have an account with your bank. And here is my bankbook. Just take the amount from my account and credit me with the traveler's checks. If they aren't honored by American Express, you won't get hurt."

"Thank you," Hillel said. "But I'll cash them at the Express office."

"Not necessary," Krensky protested, and turned to the manager. "Dr. Mondoro is a friend of mine. He is a well-known research scientist from California. I was present when he bought the checks at the airport in Los Angeles."

"We will cash them, of course," Lindtquist said, returning the bankbook to Krensky, "but I am responsible for mistakes at my bank, so please understand my caution. Pay this gentleman, Olsen."

The teller counted out thin blue hank notes and Hillel thanked him.

Krensky walked beside him as he left the building.

"What are you doing in Copenhagen, Dr. Mondoro?" he asked amicably, obviously forgetting that Hillel had introduced himself as Hauser only a few hours ago.

Hillel reacted with a fury he could not control and which surprised him. "It's none of your business! You tell that to Slaughter. Trail somebody else, Krensky."

The man no longer looked as young as before. His face became taut and his voice brittle.

"Don't make it difficult for me, Mondoro! Dr. Cory will be here soon. Then we can all return to Los Angeles. Until then I have to stay with you."

"Get lost," Hillel said.

Krensky's voice suddenly turned deep and menacing. "They're very interested in you in Washington. I don't know why, but there it is, and I'm responsible for your safety."

"Go to hell," Hillel said, and walked into the street, his teeth chattering with cold. He went into a shop and bought himself a heavy winter coat. The warmth of the thick coat helped to calm him. Without looking back, he walked on; he didn't care if Krensky followed him.

Walking down Gammal Street, he suddenly stopped, as if a

wall had risen before him. He knew that house well: there was only one front window to each floor, but the house was two rooms deep, with a kitchen on the ground floor, half below the street level. The rooms, he knew, were filled with old furniture made of teakwood, polished to a high gloss. A tiled stove stood in every room, some round, others square, the tiles painted with pictures of country scenes and blue horses.

As Hillel stared up at the windows, behind which stretched the shadowy rooms that he seemed to know so well, his hands sank deeply into his pockets, the nails dug into his palms with an excitement he could not understand.

From the green copper tower of the church came a single chime.

The echo of the bell was still in the air when a heavyset man left the house. His face looked familiar to Hillel, though he had him visualized as slim as a dancer. But he recognized his walk: one shoulder slightly lifted, the other pushing forward as though shoving obstacles out of his way. Supporting himself on a cane, the man walked on leisurely but with purpose.

That short walk down Gammal Street to the Fiskehuset restaurant had always been taken at half past twelve: it was a ritual Hillel remembered. He followed the man past century-old houses until he went through the doorway of number 34, walked through a porch, and turned to the right.

Hillel stopped. In the basement of the house a door opened into a fish shop; steps led down to a display of shrimps, smoked salmon, bundles of black eels, tin basins of oysters floating on ice. *"Artidens Fiskearter"* was painted in black letters across the door.

He knew now why he had stopped over in Copenhagen

His *Doppelgänger* was hiding behind an impregnable disguise, unassailable, like the Invisible Man. Nobody knew Hillel's face, nor that behind it he possessed Hauser's memory.

"Twenty-eight years old—wearing another face..." he

thought, aware of his power. Hauser might have been his age when he knew the man.

As if he had been waiting for a painful decision that now had been made for him, Hillel went through the porch into a small court overgrown with red ivy and up a few steps into a restaurant. An old man took his coat, repeating the word *"tack tack"* like a clock.

"This table, sir?" said a waiter.

"I always sat over there," Hillel said, walking toward the one where the man he had followed was sitting. Familiar photographs of Copenhagen, yellowed with age, hung on the walls with prints of lighthouses and ships in danger. The same lobster shell Hillel remembered hung over a doorway concealed by a curtain, as did the old clock in a corner, blending with the dark paneling. The room was filled with quiet diners, all businessmen.

Hillel sat down at the table adjoining that of his quarry, who was discussing a wine with an old waiter.

"I can recommend it, Herr Van Kungen," the waiter said. "I've never had a bottle that was *attaque.*"

Van Kungen had thrown back his head to read the wine list, looking through a pince-nez which he held like a magnifying glass. His face looked dissipated; he ate and drank too much. His hair, streaked with gray, was carefully groomed. On his right hand he wore a ring that Hillel recognized: a heavy gold ring with a blue stone on which the head of a deer was embossed.

It was the ring he had seen in his dream!

Looking at the menu without reading it, Hillel chose a dish at random and ordered half a bottle of wine. Waiting to be served, Van Kungen took a newspaper from his pocket and studied it through his pince-nez. He looked contented, a man who had created a routine for himself and had no desire to change it.

Watching the middle-aged man at the table next to his, Hillel's mind floated. Memories arose, pictures and words rolled past him kaleidoscopically. He knew he was Hauser and did not fight that; he now watched himself with scientific curiosity, registering his impressions in order to be able to give Cory a detailed report.

"Interesting ring you have," Hillel said, and bent forward to look at Van Kungen's hand. Van Kungen looked up, startled, then seeing it was a strange young man who had spoken, lifted his hand for Hillel to see.

"It's a fraternity ring, isn't it?"

"Yes, it's the crest of the Kursachsen, a student fraternity."

"May I have a look at it?"

"I haven't taken it off in twenty-odd years," Van Kungen said. "It's half grown into the flesh."

"You must've been slimmer then."

"Of course," Van Kungen answered amicably, "one cannot help putting on weight as one gets older."

The waiter brought him his soup. Ritually Van Kungen unfolded the linen napkin and stuffed a corner of it into his waistcoat.

"Remember who gave you the ring, and when?"

"Why, are you interested in jewelry?"

"No, just in this particular ring."

The waiter put a dish in front of Hillel without his noticing it.

"It's just a ring, nothing extraordinary," Van Kungen said shortly, to terminate the discussion.

"It belonged to Karl Hauser, didn't it?"

Van Kungen's eyes widened in sudden fear. "Hauser!"

"Karl Hellmuth Hauser," Hillel said, now carefully dissecting the fish on his plate.

"How do you know?" Van Kungen had forgotten his meal. His face had taken on a pallid hue patched with unhealthy red; veins bulged from his forehead.

"It was in Peenemunde, remember?"

"Peenemunde? I was never in Peenemunde," Van Kungen stammered. "Peenemunde? No."

"Then he might've given it to you here in Copenhagen. You used to sit at this table with Hauser when Denmark was occupied by the Germans." Hillel looked around the room, at the guests talking in subdued tones. "Nothing much has changed. That old waiter who served you was already old when he served you and Hauser."

Van Kungen stared at this ghost of the past. If Hillel had been older, he could possibly understand, but this man was young....

"Sven has been working in this restaurant for as long as I've been coming here." Van Kungen pushed away the bowl of soup, his appetite gone. "But who are you?"

"Hauser's memory," Hillel said, and grinned.

"That doesn't make sense. Hauser is dead. He died many years ago in the war. You could have been only a child when he died. Did you know him?"

"No. I only saw him when he was dead."

"Then he couldn't have told you anything about his past." This was a trick, Van Kungen decided; it was mysterious, but it had an explanation.

"He didn't talk to me. But I'm able to recall every moment of his life."

"You must be mad. I don't know what you want. Hauser was my closest friend, and I'm certainly not going to let you make some sort of joke of him."

He pulled back his soup bowl and started to sip, turning away from Hillel.

"He was your friend," Hillel said, "and believed in your friendship, or he wouldn't have trusted you the way he did. You're a Dane, he was a German. He had nobody else he could turn to when he was in danger."

Van Kungen made a move to get up.

"Better stay and listen," Hillel said. "You can't run away, you know. I know too much about you, Van Kungen!"

Van Kungen raised his pince-nez and studied Hillel with hard eyes, but his mouth was slack.

"There were circumstances I could not control," he said. His voice was low; it could be heard by nobody but Hillel. "I couldn't tell Karl. I would now if he were alive."

"He was until a few days ago. If he were not dead, he would be here himself, I'm sure. He couldn't get out of Russia. You knew that."

"No, I didn't, I was sure he was dead."

"I'm here in his place," Hillel said. Memory flowed into his consciousness: "You had something to give to Hauser's wife, Anna. Why didn't you?"

"I really don't know why I should continue this ridiculous farce. I don't know who you are and what your object is. But whatever it is, you can't blackmail me."

"I didn't use that word, you did." Hillel said. "But I'm glad you did. You worked with the Germans, but nobody ever found out. You were a collaborator. You'll be hanged for it."

"You look Jewish." Van Kungen's face looked apoplectic. "Maybe you're one of those Jewish murderers who roam the world to stir up trouble about the past. Maybe you're a member of the organization that kidnapped Eichmann. I'm going to call the police. This is a free country, Mr...."

"Hillel Mondoro."

"That sounds Jewish to me," Van Kungen said. "Fortunately my conscience is clear."

"Hauser gave you money to give to his wife," Hillel continued relentlessly. "Just before he was taken to a concentration camp, he turned gold and foreign currency over to you. He wanted to know that she would be safe if Germany collapsed. Since you were a Dane and his friend, he trusted you with it.

You were not suspect, but he was."

"Anna is dead. How can I give money to a dead person?" Van Kungen asked, his voice still lower.

"You never tried to find her. You used that money to make yourself a fortune. You had gold and dollars and pounds—which you had embezzled."

Van Kungen started to lift his glass to his lips, but his hand trembled and he spilled some of the wine.

"And then you denounced Hauser to the Germans. You told them he was involved in the anti-Hitler plot. He was tortured and they castrated him. Now you're sitting here, still enjoying his money."

"Air!" Van Kungen gasped, putting his hand to his heart. He was green in the face. Stumblingly he got up.

The old waiter was at his side in a moment, supporting him. "What's wrong, sir?" he asked anxiously.

"Just help me get outside," Van Kungen muttered. "I'll be all right."

Hillel threw a few bank notes on the table. He picked up his coat and walked after Van Kungen, who was taking feeble, cautious steps.

"Just leave me here." Van Kungen leaned against the wall in the small courtyard. "I'll be all right."

"Are you sure?" the waiter said. "I could call a doctor."

"No ... it's not the first time ... it'll pass," Van Kungen whispered.

"I'll stay with him," Hillel said. "I know where Herr Van Kungen lives. Just leave him with me."

Traffic roared by outside. Again one stroke of the bell came from the church tower.

"You're still here?" Van Kungen muttered.

"If Hauser were here he would have asked for an accounting, and he would've turned you over to the Danish police."

"I didn't know Anna had survived the war. I'd have made

good." He kept his hand pressed against his chest. "Just leave me alone."

"You never even tried to find out if Hauser was alive."

"Where should I have started to look? He disappeared in a concentration camp."

"You put him there!"

"That's a lie." Van Kungen set his heavy body into motion, walking close to the brick wall, and made for the street.

Hillel walked beside him, listening to the man's heavy breathing. He felt no regret or compassion, only relief as if he had accomplished what he had wanted to do for years. But at the same time he was aware of being a spectator watching the result of an experiment like a researcher watching a laboratory test on animal behavior. A second consciousness seemed to work in him, and he repeated to himself inaudibly, "I must not forget. I must observe. I must report to Cory."

"I will look for Anna. Or do you have her address?" Van Kungen said. "I'll make good. It isn't too late. Anna was very dear to me. I didn't forget about her on purpose."

Hillel did not answer. They had reached the bank where Hillel had cashed his check.

"I'll give you money for her," Van Kungen said. "And if you tell me where I can find her, I'll go and see her and look after her."

Laboriously Van Kungen climbed the few steps into the bank.

"Call Lindtquist," he said to the teller, leaning against the counter, his face covered with sweat.

The teller gave Hillel a startled look and disappeared, to return with the monocled manager.

"I need twenty thousand German marks in notes," Van Kungen said to Lindtquist. "Not in a check."

"I don't know if we have that much cash on hand, Herr Van Kungen," the manager said, watching Hillel suspiciously. Maybe the man had a gun on his client.

"Then make up the rest in dollars and pounds," Van Kungen said. "Anything but Danish currency."

"Are you sure you want it that way?" Lindtquist tried to stall. "And is this man with you?"

"Yes, yes." Van Kungen raised his voice. "Give me the money, quick!"

"Of course." Lindtquist motioned to the teller, who opened a drawer of foreign bank notes and started calculating on an adding machine. "I'll write up the receipt. Twenty thousand German marks or its equivalent in foreign exchange."

"That'll keep her until I hear from you," Van Kungen said to Hillel. His breathing had become more labored.

Lindtquist started to count the notes on the counter.

"Just put it into an envelope," Van Kungen said. "and let me get out of here." Opening a small silver box, he popped some pills into his mouth.

Lindtquist, still baffled, pushed a receipt over to Van Kungen.

"Take that to her," Van Kungen said, passing the envelope to Hillel, who slid it into his pocket. "And let me have her address as soon as possible."

"I will," Hillel said. He turned and walked away. He did not know where Anna Hauser lived but was sure he would find her when the moment presented itself.

In the doorway stood Krensky.

As Hillel walked down the steps into the street, he heard a scream of pain and the sound of a heavy body hitting the floor.

"Call a doctor! An ambulance!" he heard Lindtquist shout.

Hillel walked along Gammal Street and turned toward the church tower. The street widened into a square bordered by greenery. *"Hojbro,"* the street sign read. A policeman wearing white cuffs over his sleeves was directing traffic.

"What did you do to that man?" Krensky was at Hillel's side.

"Are you still around?" Hillel turned to him threateningly. "I told you to get lost."

"Why did he give you all that money?"

"That's what interests you most, money! You'd sell out for money, to anybody, wouldn't you? How much would you take to get out of my sight for good?"

He was looking at the church. As if layers of consciousness unpeeled themselves in his memory, he remembered its name: St. Nicholas' Church on Nicolij Plads. How often had this church entered his mind? His mind? Hauser's mind? The two consciousnesses were intermixed, but he felt a deep relief: he had finally accomplished something he had turned over in his mind many thousands of times. Van Kungen's death was an accomplished fact.

Hillel felt elated. The depression that had pressed against him like a vise had disappeared. He could not remember having been so happy in a long time. Manic-depressive, he noted. He must tell Cory.

But whose emotions was he experiencing? Could they be his own?

15

"I can't return with you right now," Hillel said. "I can't! I haven't finished...."

Despite the near-darkness, Cory had not turned on the lights in the hotel room. The evening sun, enormous in an azure sky, shone on Hillel's face with a ghostly light.

"What do you have to finish?" Cory asked. Hillel seemed to be on the verge of nervous exhaustion.

"I should be able to distinguish which thought is mine and which is Hauser's, but the foreign influence in my body throws off my judgment."

"Let me be the judge," Cory said. "Get your things ready. We'll take the night plane to California."

"No!"

Hillel's refusal was threatening, vicious. Cory turned on the lights.

"You know, for a moment you looked as if you wanted to attack me. Nothing has happened that can really hurt you, and nothing will as long as we are together. If you want to stay in Europe a few days longer, I'll stay with you; but how can we explain to Karen why we haven't taken the next plane back?"

Cory tried to sound convincing, but the truth was that everything was working out perfectly. He wanted Hillel to continue to respond to the influence of Hauser's RNA, free from Slaughter's questions and Karen's presence.

"Tell her I must go to Berlin," Hillel said.

"Why Berlin?"

Hillel took out the envelope with Van Kungen's money and scattered the contents over Cory's bed.

"I must deliver this."

"To whom?"

"To Hauser's wife." Hillel sat down on the bed. "He wanted

to see her. Now, since he's dead, it's my duty to carry on for him. This has nothing to do with Karen, or you, or the experiment. I killed Van Kungen, and that puts me under an obligation."

"You didn't kill him. And you are obliged to no one. You can mail that money and stop playing Hauser." Cory was watching Hillel narrowly. "Or is there still another reason why you want to go to Germany?"

"I don't want to discuss it," Hillel said coldly. "I'm going. It doesn't matter if I stay a day or two longer, does it? Or do you want me to run out on you again?"

It seemed impossible to reestablish the old contact between them.

"How much do you remember about Hauser?"

Hillel shut his lips tight and turned his head toward the window, avoiding Cory's eyes.

"I see," said Cory with deliberate toughness. "You might as well admit that you've given up working with me and that you want to pursue Hauser's ideas, whatever they were, on your own. Why don't you cooperate? Is there some reason you refuse to talk about Hauser?"

"No."

"Good. What was his job in Russia?"

"He was a mathematician and experimented with electromagnetism as a method of controlling hydrogen explosions. It was his idea, and he was well advanced in his thinking."

"You know his ... thinking? Can you recall the formulas he was working on?"

Hillel glanced suspiciously at Cory. "Why do you ask me that?"

"Because that's what Slaughter wants to know. Just because we haven't seen him lately, don't think he isn't around. You're much too important for him not to keep track of every step you take. I'm sure he knows that you're visiting me. I wouldn't be surprised if this room is bugged."

"And if it is? He won't learn anything. Are you questioning me because Slaughter wants to know? Maybe you're pumping me on purpose, feeding what I say into his microphone. I thought you were only interested in the RNA experiment, Cory." His voice roughened. "Did Slaughter buy you too?"

"You know I'm not interested in Slaughter," Cory said carefully. It was like being confronted by a dangerous animal that would attack immediately if it smelled fear. "I must know all that is to be known about Hauser, his intentions, how and when his memory appears in your mind. Is there a distinction between your memory and his? Can you separate them? I've observed that some questions of mine aggravate you, questions which you, Hillel, would not resent, but which Hauser might."

"Like what?" Hillel suddenly seemed to relax, his hostility evaporated.

"Whenever I ask about Hauser's plans and why he wanted to leave Russia, I find you on the defensive. Why? Can't you keep his personality and yours apart?"

Hillel looked at him reflectively.

"I am in full control of my will," he said finally. "I had one shock, that was when I left for Copenhagen. There are moments that I can't remember. But I was not prepared for such an eventuality. Now I am. But hasn't the idea struck you that Hauser might have been a monomaniac, a pathological case? If that's so, his actions would be erratic. No pattern for them could be found."

"What actions?"

"Desires anchored in his past, which now would come to the fore. I can't give you an example," Hillel said reluctantly, as if forcing himself to talk.

"I don't believe that Hauser was a paranoiac. If he was, we'll never find out."

"You will, by my actions," Hillel said, moving closer to Cory.

He talked in a whisper, as if he were afraid a third person might be listening.

"Let's examine his case. He was kept a prisoner in Russia. He was treated well. He even had a country house, a *dacha,* which only a few select persons are permitted to have. He made a comfortable living and was an important man. But he resented being kept against his will in Baikonur. He wanted to see his wife again and his son. Also some people who had done him great harm."

"Who were those people?"

Hillel stopped, as if suddenly pained by that alien memory.

"Listen," Cory said, dry and authoritative, "talk to me as Hillel Mondoro. Ask yourself if you don't want to defy the purpose of our experiment—because Hauser wants it to fail."

Hillel stared at Cory, as though to draw from him all the strength he needed, and took a deep breath, trying to overcome a mental hurdle. But his face slipped into a mask which Cory knew he could not dislodge.

"I don't know," Hillel said sullenly.

"You're keeping things from me," Cory said.

"I told you I don't know," Hillel said, suddenly furious.

His lie was confirmation. Cory knew he was witnessing a breakthrough in science. If the Hauser-Mondoro case developed as he expected, if it was possible to transfer not only memory but also personality traits, then he might have found the key to immortality. A landscape of unsolved questions spread out before him, vast, limitless. Cory felt that he had pried open the door to a new universe; but he knew that he could not stop at the threshold.

"Why did Hauser leave?" Cory asked, vainly knocking at Hillel's closed mind.

"I don't know. Please ask no more questions." His eyes widened. "I must see Anna."

"Anna?"

"That's his wife's name. Names appear clearly in my mind. Situations are sometimes surrounded by a kind of —fog ... they're blurred ... or they take shape, come into focus. I can visualize a tall, very handsome blonde young woman. Powerful. Very Nordic. He was dependent on her, and she was the dominant factor in his life."

"Does your memory tell you this, or is it conjecture based on that picture in your mind?" Cory asked

How deeply had memory cut itself into Hillel's brain? It even seemed to reproduce emotions.

"I must see her." It was Hauser speaking.

"All right," Cory said. "If it's so important to you, let's fly to Berlin. Your actions are links in the chain of your observations."

Hillel looked at him searchingly. "I never realized it before, but you're cold-blooded."

"So were you where your work was concerned, Hillel. If we let emotions interfere with our observations, we'll never arrive at unbiased results."

Hillel suddenly clasped his hands over his face. "I don't want to go back ever!"

Overcome by emotion, he got up quickly and walked heavily to the window. From the hotel's height, he looked down at the city, at the green gardens of the Tivoli bathed in still greener artificial lights, at the spire of the town hall.

Fascinated by the spectacle of this Jekyll-and-Hyde personality swinging from Mondoro to Hauser and back again, Cory asked with deliberate cruelty to evoke Hillel Mondoro: "What about Karen?"

"Karen?" Hillel looked blankly at Cory. It was as if he had forgotten that a woman called Karen existed.

"I know. I will go back to her, but ... there are things I must do first. I won't be ... free until then." He had to search for words to convey his thoughts to Cory. "I believe that Hauser

wanted to ... return to the past ... that his desires about what
he wanted to do were limited. He had a few main objectives.
But none beyond them."

"And you want to fulfill them?"

"I have to. I'm convinced that after that I'll regain my freedom of choice."

"Have you lost it?"

"No. But I must get his memory out of my system or I don't
think I could ever be as happy as before." Suddenly the color
returned to his face, and his eyes became lively and alert, as if
Hauser's memory had vanished. "Karen wouldn't accept me,
if I don't get Hauser out of my system. That's why I must carry
out what Hauser had in mind. Feed him his own ideas until
they dry up. Only one thing can kill him, and that is the fulfill-
ment of his manic ideas."

16

Anna Hauser lived in the Bernauerstrasse in West Berlin.

Opposite her two small rooms in a dilapidated apartment house stood the Wall, which divided Berlin into the zone of the DDR, the German Democratic Republic, and the zone of the DBR, the German Federal Republic. The apartment houses on the eastern side looked two-dimensional. with bricked-us windows, concrete blocks and barbed wire where formerly there had been gardens. The entrances to the houses were boarded up, the paint on the walls had faded. They looked pale and corpselike. The word "Murderer" was written in large white letters across a wall, and on the sidewalk outside the house stood a simple cross of slim birch branches nailed together. On its horizontal bar was carved the name of the man who had jumped from the roof of the house: "Bernd Lunser, driven to his death by the *Volkspolizei.* He died for freedom." Around the cross barbed wire was hung like a crown of thorns.

Anna Hauser had been in those two little rooms in the attic since the day the Americans had occupied West Berlin. Here she wanted to stay for the rest of her days, doing penance for Germany's shame. Since the end of the war she had worn black, not because she was mourning for her husband, Karl Hellmuth Hauser, or for the worldly possessions she had lost, or for her former social standing. She was mourning the demise of the Greater Reich.

From below her attic windows she could watch the crowd of curious sightseers staring at the stone wall, this monument of shame. Foreign soldiers with cameras, tourists with cameras, trucks filled with workmen taking pictures, buses and cars bursting with people came to photograph the Wall, gaping, laughing, strewing about the remains of sandwiches and wax paper, guzzling beer, acting as if they were at a carnival.

Anna did some work for a shop on Kurfurstendamm, the fashionable main street of West Berlin. She had done knitting in her happier days and also during the war, making muffs for women and coats for soldiers sacrificing their lives for the Führer on the wintry Russian front. Now her skill was keeping her alive. Her knitted dresses, for which she received little money, were bought by rich foreigners, Jews probably, who took them home to their countries as booty from subjugated Germany.

She rarely looked into the large mirror in her living room, put there for women who came for fittings. She paid no attention to her grayish, faded hair, which still had traces of the color of wheat, a color that once had made her face glow. Now she dragged her hair back harshly into a thick knot, exposing her pale face with its hard square chin in which the misery of life had carved indelible lines. Hers was a burned-out face, still betraying a former Valkyrie beauty.

Once a week she traveled to the Kurfürstendamm, where she went into a fashionable store by the back door to deliver the week's labor and receive money that bore not the picture of the Führer but a scarecrow drawing of the disarmed German eagle.

One day Anna discovered an exhibition about Auschwitz, the extermination camp, and made repeated visits to look at the pictures of the *Leichengraben*—the trenches filled with corpses—at the ovens belching black smoke, at pictures of human skeletons in tattered shirts, fleshless, the noses large, the mouths caved in. Those were the enemies who had destroyed Germany in the end. The Führer had been right to exterminate them, but he had not been able to get them all. Those who had escaped had treacherously thrust the dagger into Germany's back. Anna was sorry when the exhibition was moved to another city. The visits to the Auschwitz exhibition were exhilarating. She had lost no time from work; she had taken her knitting needles along.

Like the Führer who had been betrayed by his people, she too had been betrayed. Her son Dieter was an actor in the Eastern zone of Berlin, a Communist, an enemy of Greater Germany. Karl, her husband, was working for the Russians, applying his talents, his knowledge and his skills, which he had been taught in German universities, to the Mongol people, who like Genghis Khan had overrun Germany, raped women, burned houses, committed atrocities about which she dared not think.

Anna put her black scarf over her faded hair and picked up a cardboard box containing a newly made dress and her knitting basket, so as not to lose time while traveling to the Kurfurstendamm.

She walked down Tauentzinstrasse, crossed into the back entrance of the House of Knitting, delivered her goods, received a new order and hastened toward the bus station that took her home.

"Mrs. Hauser?" a man said at her side.

The stranger was dark-skinned, his hair wavy, his face long, his eyes Mediterranean black, like one of those slave workers during the war. He was one of the despicable breed that traveled Germany, their pockets filled with money, sleeping with shameless blonde German girls.

"Yes," she said warily.

"I have a message for you," Hillel said.

"A message?"

"Shall we go over there and discuss it?" Hillel suggested, indicating a small bar.

Only now did he look closely at Anna. He had visualized her as Hauser had seen her last: a blonde Nordic beauty, with soft breasts and an abandon that stimulated intense desire, a desire that his mutilation had made al most unbearable. Now the haunting picture of this older woman imprinted itself in

Hillel's mind, overlaying Hauser's memory of her.

"I don't know you," Anna said.

"I bring regards from a friend of yours, from Copenhagen. From Dag Van Kungen. He asked me to look you up."

It had not been difficult to find her. Lying in bed in his room at the Savoy in the Fasanenstrasse, images had come to him as if reeled off by a motion picture projector. Hauser knew her habits intimately.

"Dag?" she said incredulously. "I haven't heard from him since the end of the war. How is he?"

A sudden excitement colored her cheeks. She smiled, revealing two rows of impeccable teeth that had never been touched by a dentist's drill.

"Mr. Van Kungen asked me to invite you for a drink, and he gave me something for you."

"Dag," she repeated, savoring the name. "All right. Let's go to Mampe. That's where we sometimes met before it got bombed out."

They crossed the street.

"Dag took care of me when Karl was arrested," she said.

She walked beside Hillel, taller than he, her feet clad in strong shoes, the heels low, the leather coarse. She wore wrinkled cotton stockings. Silently they passed the Kaiser Wilhelm Gedächtnis Church, its clock stopped eternally at twenty-five past one, the time when the bomb had struck, passed garden restaurants with gay awnings and heat lamps shining like small yellow moons to chase away the cold. Streams of people flooded by, and the traffic moved slowly and noisily, yellow double-decker buses, automobiles, almost bumper to bumper, directed by weaponless traffic police in white coats.

The Mampe Stube was dark, and her eyes needed time to adjust themselves to the artificial light. The paneled room was almost empty. She refused to take off her coat; like her clothes it was made of leftover yarn.

"And why didn't Dag get in touch with me himself?" she asked.

"He didn't know where to look for you," Hillel said.

"Is he married?"

"He didn't have a woman with him when I saw him."

The answer seemed to cheer her. "How did you know where to find me? Where did you meet Dag? You don't talk with a foreign accent. You are not German either. Who are you?" The questions tumbled from her lips.

"He gave me money for you," Hillel said. "Twenty thousand German marks."

"Why?"

"He owes them to you, he told me. And should you need anything ..." Hillel stopped. Van Kungen was not alive anymore.

"He owes me much, but not money," Anna said.

Hillel took out the manila envelope bulging with bank notes. "He wants you to have this."

"I don't understand," she answered blankly, staring at the fortune before her. "I have no claim to this money."

A waiter was standing patiently at the table.

"Coffee," Anna said.

"Two," Hillel said to the waiter. "Anything else?"

Anna ignored his question. "Why did Dag desert me?"

"I told you, he didn't know where to find you all those years."

"And he gave you money for me? Does he know you that well ... are you related to him?"

"It isn't his money," Hillel said. "Your husband gave it to him for you before he was arrested."

"He kept it for so many years?" It did not make sense to her, nor did it fit the image of Van Kungen she had carefully preserved in her mind. "I don't want that money."

"But it's yours," Hillel urged.

"I won't take money from Karl."

"Karl Hauser gave Van Kungen gold and foreign exchange which he had saved for the day when the German mark might become worthless. He knew about inflation, having lived through it before."

"This is Judas money. It should have belonged to the German Reich. With that money Karl betrayed his fatherland, as he betrays it now, working for the Russians."

"He is dead," Hillel said. "Your husband is dead."

Anna looked at him unmoved. "For me he died many years ago. I will never cry for him. Those Russian Mongols kept him fat, bribed him to work for them. He slept with their women. He committed treason against his race, betrayed his Aryan blood in Russian bordellos, made bastard children with slit-eyed whores from Mongolia."

Hillel saw the gleam of insanity in her destroyed face. There was no way to approach her; not even Van Kungen could have found one. But he was elated that one more of Hauser's tasks now lay behind him.

"Are you related to Dag?" she asked suspiciously. "You didn't answer my question."

"No. My name is Hillel Mondoro and I live in California. But won't you take this money? I can't give it back to Van Kungen."

"Why not?"

"He is dead."

Anna sat motionless, her face gray.

"He must have been dead for years," she said finally. "I'm sure he must have died years ago, or he would have found me."

Her blue eyes glittered, and her voice was dry and sharp.

"Give the money to Dieter. He takes alms from his father. You say Karl is dead? Well, he died for me on the twentieth of June, nineteen forty-four, when that bomb he hoped would murder the Führer exploded and with it Germany's future."

"He had nothing to do with that," Hillel said. "Van Kungen denounced him."

Anna rose to her feet. "Dag? Never! Karl should have been garroted like the other traitors. But he saved himself by running over to the Russians. Did he really believe I would accept this blood money? How little he ever knew me. Did he think I would sell out my faith for money? I hope he died the hard way."

She walked off, a tall woman with traces of a beauty which age and privation could not completely destroy.

Hillel looked around the small bar beginning to fill with people who talked a language that he spoke but that he had never learned. He had another picture of Germany in his mind—Hauser's idealistic concept of it. Hauser had known the Germany that hated common sense and intelligence, that imposed "soul conformity." But below the noisy surface of Nazism there had been the silent, tough, unconquerable opposition of a part of the nation to which Hauser was proud to belong. In his exile he had pictured a new Germany, where people like himself would be spiritual and scientific leaders, since science and spirituality were indivisible for him. But the faces in the Mampe bar and in the streets were faces like Anna's, unapproachable by reason, no different from the people Hauser had known thirty years ago.

There was no such land as Hauser had dreamed about, to which he had wanted to bring his Promethean gift.

Aware of thoughts that had not germinated in his own mind, Hillel shivered with sudden fear. On the napkin he had drawn ornate letters, not in his handwriting but in Gothic German:

$$\mathfrak{J}.\mathfrak{M}.\mathfrak{U}.$$

Were they initials of a name? Hillel repeated the three letters until they blurred into a sentence: I am you. It was the devil speaking to him.

In sudden panic he got up, threw some money on the table,

and followed by the startled eyes of the people in the bar, ran out into the street.

The traffic noise hit him like a scream. He kept on running, past Joachimsthalerstrasse, past the Hotel Kempinsky, only to stop at a building that displayed a six-cornered star—the Star of David. It was a synagogue. Hillel tried to open the door, but it was locked. The Catholics keep their churches open all the time, he thought, for people who feel in need of prayer. Should prayer be restricted to certain times? He shook the heavy door; it did not give way. But would he find answer and solace in this house?

He crossed the street to his hotel. It was one of the few buildings that had not been gutted by bombs. The doorman pushed open the wide glass door for him. The lobby was quiet. He picked up his key.

"Dr. Mondoro," the clerk said. "Dr. Cory would like to see you as soon as you come in. He's in his room."

17

"Why do you travel so much, Dr. Mondoro?" Slaughter said, smiling wryly.

He, Cory, and Krensky were sitting around a small table facing the door. An ashtray was heaped with half-smoked cigarettes. Krensky's round face wore an expression of irritation and discomfort. Cory watched the other men as if through a window.

"Did you ask me to your room to meet these CIA people?" Hillel asked indignantly.

"You alone are responsible for your present condition," Slaughter said in a dry lawyer's voice. "Don't blame us. You got us in trouble. You stole something and we want it back."

"What are you talking about?" Hillel said with suppressed fury.

"Hauser's memory. We didn't choose you, we never would have. Why don't you sit down and talk civilly with us? After all, I flew six thousand miles to see you."

"To hell with you," Hillel said.

Cory had never seen him like this, the lips thin, the skin under his eyes sagging. He looked like a man twice his age. This was not Dr. Hillel Mondoro, a man balanced in his emotions, trained to think logically, slowly, methodically, never given to sudden outbursts, never aggressive. Behind that dark-skinned face hid a hurt, savage creature, ready to attack.

"I insist that you return with us to Washington," Slaughter said. "We must know what you know. You stole a man's memory. We want that memory, that's all. Then you're on your own again."

"If I knew what you want to know and if I told you," Hillel said, and his grin froze into a snarl, "I'd spend the rest of my life behind bars."

"Don't be ridiculous," Slaughter interjected. "How could we send you to prison? On what charge?"

"There're bars in a lunatic asylum too. You'll have me declared insane and dangerous. That can easily be accomplished, Slaughter. You'd keep me in solitary confinement to the end of my days."

"You *are* insane," Slaughter said.

"I know that's your opinion, and you'd be even more convinced I'm mad *after I* talked. You'd keep me from seeing anybody, even my wife, afraid that I might give away information that you believe I'm keeping from you purposely. In the name of your country's security, you feel you can excuse any kind of action."

"Your imagination is running away with you," Slaughter said, composing himself. "You're a citizen of a free country. I'm sure you're sensible enough to come with us of your own free will. Why shouldn't you? Many people in our government are sworn to secrecy and stick to it all their lives. Why should you be an exception, Dr. Mondoro? There's nothing in your files that shows you're not a loyal citizen. Don't talk like a martyr. We'll do anything you want us to do: give you a job, build you a lab, finance any research, pay you a pension—anything. Just name it. All we want is your goodwill."

"Now all you have to do to prove your sincerity is produce a gun," Hillel said.

Without a word, Krensky put a small pistol on the table. It was thick in the middle and looked as if it could shoot a flare.

"Slaughter!" Cory sprang up in alarm. "This has gone far enough. Tell your man to put that thing away."

"He can't force me to return with him, Dottore," Hillel said.

"We're getting nowhere." Slaughter got up impatiently. "We'll take Dr. Mondoro to the plane, and I'm sure he'll be reasonable. This isn't an ordinary gun, Cory. It shoots only tranquilizers. I hate to use this sort of device. Why don't we act intelligently and not emotionally? What's your decision?"

Krensky picked up the gun and turned it contemplatively in his pudgy hands.

"I must go to East Berlin," Hillel said desperately. "I must! It will take only an hour, and then I'll come with you."

"If you cross that border you'll never get out," Slaughter said. "I'm sure the Russians know about Dr. Cory's experiment by now. They're bound to try and get hold of you. Once in the Eastern zone, they'd have you, wouldn't they? And they're even less choosy in their methods than we are. No, I can't let you go."

"Why East Berlin?" Krensky spoke for the first time. "Couldn't somebody else go for you and do whatever you have to do?"

Hillel did not answer, and turned as if he wanted to leave the room. "Are you going to put me in a trunk like the Egyptians did when they shipped that double agent from Italy to Cairo?"

"Please, be sensible," Slaughter said. "I have no choice."

"Nor have I," Hillel said.

At that moment Krensky shot him. A small pin penetrated his coat sleeve. Hillel looked perplexed and pulled it out. A glassy look came into his eyes. Quickly Krensky walked up to him and supported him.

"He won't collapse," Slaughter said to Cory. "But he will be quite docile for a while. We have excellent scientists working for us, especially chemists," he said with a twinkle. "Let's go. Mondoro's bill's paid, his luggage is in the lobby. I'd like you to come along too, Dr. Cory."

Krensky walked Hillel to the door. He offered no resistance.

"I'm a lawyer, brought up to hate violence," Slaughter said. "I'm sorry for what I had to do."

A taxi was waiting at the hotel entrance. The porter had loaded the suitcases into the trunk.

For a moment Cory was relieved that Slaughter had taken

the initiative. He longed for the security of his laboratory, sharing Slaughter's dislike of violence. Once back home, he could observe Hillel's condition under controlled circumstances.

The taxi drove off. Krensky was sitting next to the chauffeur, a young man with a sharp, alert face, smoking a cigarette which dangled from the corner of his mouth.

"Tempelhof," Slaughter ordered.

"I know," the driver replied without turning.

"The East Germans make it quite difficult for any West Berliner to get to the Tempelhof airport. They make them drive around East Berlin in a half-circle."

Cory moved farther into his corner as Hillel's body pressed heavily against him. Hillel's eyes were half closed and his breath left his mouth spasmodically. Cory watched Hillel with concern. Was he still conducting a scientific experiment, or had he involved himself in a criminal act?

"You leave yourself open to a nice charge of kidnapping." Cory said, his uneasiness trying to find an outlet. "Mondoro is a free agent and has nothing to do with your organization."

"The word *agent* has many meanings," Slaughter said facetiously. I'm going to deliver this young man, healthy and in good physical condition, to Dr. Wendtland and let him solve the legal questions. But I don't think it will come to that. I'm just doing what I'm ordered to do. Our business can't be measured by ordinary standards. Yours can't either. If you followed only the established law, you'd never arrive at new results. Laws are not written for exceptions."

Slaughter's long face suddenly looked blank.

"This isn't the way to Tempelhof," he said.

"No." Krensky turned in his seat and raised his pistol. "It isn't. We're crossing the border into East Berlin at the Potsdamer Platz."

The atmosphere of cross and double cross, of deceit and make-believe, fitted the pattern that Cory had observed since he had started the RNA experiment. Ever since the RNA had roiled the depths of Hillel's mind, waves of the upheaval had lapped toward Cory also.

Slaughter's eyes nearly disappeared into the shadowy caverns of their sockets. His lips pulled away from his long teeth, and he bent forward to stare at Krensky with silent curiosity. His pallor accentuated the thousand freckles on his face.

"The Eastern zone?" he repeated, as if he had not understood.

"You'll get out before we cross over," Krensky said. "I'm sorry."

"You're sorry," Slaughter repeated in surprise. "What are you sorry about? About your double cross? Or did Mondoro bribe you to drive him into the DDR?"

"This is ridiculous," Cory said. "How can this man take us against our will across the border? We're three against one."

"My orders are to take you along, Dr. Cory," Krensky said evenly. "And also Dr. Mondoro. Don't do anything foolish or I'll have to use my gun. Dr. Mondoro is in no condition to help, Mr. Slaughter wouldn't, and the driver is one of my men."

Reacting to his name, Hillel opened his eyes, his forehead furrowed in a futile attempt to understand the situation.

"Dr. Mondoro is happy to visit the DDR." Krensky spoke slowly and hypnotically. "He demanded it, didn't you, Dr. Mondoro?"

The taxi suddenly stopped. An American convoy droned through the intersection of Lutzowplatz and Einemstrasse, jeeps mounting recoilless rifles, their snouts covered with leather caps; on one of the trucks a young, grim-looking soldier manned a heavy machine gun.

Cory bent toward the door. An anger he had never before experienced tightened the muscles in his face. He had never been physically aggressive and could not remember ever having hit anybody in anger. But to be held captive by one man aroused in him a contempt for himself.

"Don't," Slaughter warned. "Krensky won't hesitate to kill you. He's too stupid to think of the consequences. This thing has been arranged and organized. We're being followed by another car. You wouldn't get far, Cory."

The convoy clattered by and the taxi drove on.

"I haven't got the makings of a hero," Slaughter said.

"I don't think your morals are any better than Krensky's," Cory said. The opportunity to fight Krensky had passed.

"We're going to stop at the next corner," Krensky said. "You will get out, Mr. Slaughter. A car will stop close by, and you will wait at the curb until that car drives on. If you don't, you might get hurt."

"If he could, he'd kill me," Slaughter said, his face ash-gray. "But he wouldn't know what to do with my remains. It's tough to get rid of corpses. To have you kidnapped is an asset for us, Cory. We'll get you back fast. I don't think the East Germans would appreciate an international incident."

The taxi had come to a halt. Slaughter stepped out and slammed the door. The driver immediately moved on. Through the rear window Cory watched an automobile stop close to Slaughter. Four men were in it.

"Your passport, please," Krensky said. "I've already got Dr. Mondoro's."

"To hell with you," Cory said.

"In that case I must ask you to leave the car too," Krensky said. "You prefer leaving Dr. Mondoro?"

Cory threw his passport onto Krensky's seat.

There was the Wall, a grim heap of concrete blocks and snake pits of barbed wire. The taxi stopped at a barrier, and a West German policeman in a green uniform walked leisurely up to Krensky, who waved the American passports at him.

"I'm taking my guests from America sightseeing to the never-never land," Krensky joked.

The guard smiled and another opened the barrier. As the guard took the passports from Krensky and turned to the shack behind him to have them stamped, Cory jumped at Krensky.

"Stop him," he shouted.

The taxi leaped forward, scraping under the half-open barrier. Giving way to his pent-up anger, Cory hit Krensky, who rolled sideways and slid between seat and dashboard out of Cory's reach. Falling over the back of the seat, Cory grabbed the man's throat and choked him. The taxi careened and swayed and came to an abrupt stop. Its four doors were pulled open simultaneously, and half a dozen hands tore Cory away from the man on the floor. He was pulled out of the car and found himself surrounded by Vopos, the East German *Volkspolizei.*

Nursing his throat, Krensky climbed back onto his seat.

Cory was rudely pushed back into the taxi, one of the guards crowded Cory against Hillel—who had not moved and who seemed to be unaware of the scuffle—another slid in beside Krensky, and the taxi drove on, its gears whining. The whole incident had not taken more than a few seconds.

Glancing back, Cory saw a group of soldiers running toward the barrier on the West German side. two hundred feet away. The East German side was crowded with Vopos, who soon cut off the view.

"How stupid of you," Krensky said, coughing. "You could've killed us all." His moon face did not show any anger. "I didn't know you had it in you, Doctor."

Cory moved as far as he could away from the Vopo whose machine pistol was pressed painfully against his body. He smelled the sour odor of men who had been in their clothes too long.

"See what you've done," Krensky complained. "Now we've lost our good American passports!"

18

"Shepilov," the gray-haired man introduced himself, his craggy face showing lines that could have been interpreted as a smile. "I hope you find your room comfortable. May we come in?"

"Asking a prisoner if the jailer can enter his cell?" Cory asked.

The room was fairly large in a boardinghouse in East Berlin, the Pension am Friedrichs Hain. The pension covered the third floor of a large apartment house. There were offices on the first and second floors and shops at street level. An elevator was the only approach to the pension; the staircase was locked with a wrought-iron gate.

"But you're not a prisoner," Shepilov said, coming into the room.

"Then why the locked gate on the staircase?"

Shepilov looked dejected. "That's the trouble with us Russians—everything has to be secret and locked. It was no different in the czar's time. It's part of our makeup. By nature we are suspicious people."

He waved his hand at a tall man with a shock of unruly hair who had entered behind him. "Professor Vassilov of the University of Moscow."

Vassilov looked like a peasant who had come home from hard work in the fields and had been dressed up in a gray suit that did not fit him. He took Cory's hand in both of his. His merry eyes showed obvious pleasure.

"I am very happy to meet you," he boomed in a rumbling bass voice. "I've read all of your publications. They are revelations to me. I also know about your work in other fields and have wanted to meet you for a long time. But not under these circumstances."

"If we had wanted to talk to you, we wouldn't have taken

you to America by force," Cory said resentfully.

"I know, very unnecessary," Vassilov growled. "But quite beyond my power to prevent."

To hide his anger, Cory walked to the window and looked at the street below with its scant traffic. The houses opposite, still scaffolded and unoccupied, were crawling with workmen. Hundreds of new buildings had mushroomed throughout East Berlin, covering the scars of a war which, though the shooting had stopped years ago, was still smoldering.

He turned his back to the window and regarded his unopened luggage gloomily. On the table were glasses and soft drinks, German beer, and a bottle of Asbach Uralt, a German brandy. Vassilov opened the bottle and poured three glasses from it, pushing one toward Cory.

"We've been following your experiments with the greatest excitement," Vassilov said. "We've tried to repeat your tests, but failed all along the line. The nature of engram, memory trace, has remained frustratingly elusive to us. I am reminded of my mother's cooking recipes. She would willingly pass them on, but always omitted a few ingredients, just to keep her friends in the dark and remain the outstanding cook she was."

"You know very well, Professor, that the worst thing that can happen to you in science is to have others unable to repeat your experiments," Cory said. He could sense an atmosphere of danger. "Did you bring me here to have me reveal secrets that don't exist? The tests I have published contain all the details needed for repetition. Others have not been in print."

"I guessed that much," Vassilov said. "But now, since you are here, could we talk about the material that has not been printed! I'm most curious. We approached your RNA research from the opposite direction. We tried to erase memories by applying enzyme ribonuclease, which breaks down the RNA and memory banks."

"That could be a potential weapon for wiping out undesirable memories in people," Cory said.

"You too have been brainwashed, to use your expression," Shepilov said heatedly. "You too see the negative aspects in everything we do."

"Please," Vassilov interfered, "Dr. Cory has a right to mistrust us. How would you react, Ivan, if those strong-arm methods had been used on you, and you were sitting in West Berlin or Washington in a room with locked doors?"

"Dr. Cory had the choice to stay in West Berlin. Krensky offered it to him. He chose to accompany Dr. Mondoro."

"Where is he?" Cory asked.

"In the room next to yours. He is sleeping off that narcotic. When he wakes up he will be perfectly all right," Shepilov said.

"And we will witness a very important moment in your research," Vassilov added, "an empirical proof. Only empirical proof can give you the answer to your work."

Cory, his curiosity aroused, looked questioningly at him.

"Heuser knew Shepilov well. If Mondoro were to recognize him, wouldn't that be added proof that your experiment is successful?"

"It would, but all I'm interested in at the moment is returning home with Dr. Mondoro. Let me see him," Cory said impatiently. "You have no right to hold either of us."

"Your indignation is not fully justified," Vassilov answered, and emptied his glass. "To be just, you ought to look at Comrade Ivan's point of view too and recall the events that brought Dr. Mondoro here. Hauser, after all, was abducted by the CIA."

"You know he wasn't," Cory said. "For twenty years he wanted to leave Russia. You kept him by force, as you are keeping us here."

"All right, even if I accept your explanation, why was he shot by your people when he changed his mind and wanted to return to us?" Shepilov asked.

"We shot him?" said Cory exasperated. "This is the way you

operate. You make completely false statements and insist they're true until they're proved wrong. Even then you sometimes stick to them. You do the same in your science. It doesn't work that way."

"You consented to transfer Hauser's memory to another person," Shepilov said. "Why that particular man's memory? To learn, perhaps, about Hauser's work in the use of certain forces to control hydrogen explosions?"

"I consented because this was a chance for me to work on a human, and with government permission. I've nothing to do with any government agency, nor with Hauser's past, which does not concern me," Cory said, aware that he was on the defensive.

"Dr. Cory, like me, is only interested in his scientific work," Vassilov said, to smooth Cory's resentment. "Mondoro met that man in Copenhagen, Dag Van Kungen, who should have been sent to prison for collaboration with the Nazis. He visited Hauser's wife in Berlin. He did what Hauser had set out to do. That seems to be proof that Dr. Cory has succeeded in his experiment. Now Mondoro wants to meet Hauser's son here in East Berlin. We can't have enough checkups on Cory's test. I suggest that we help Mondoro as much as we can whenever he acts in accordance with Hauser's memory."

"You are well informed," Cory said. "You must've followed Mondoro from Los Angeles. But what you just said proves that you didn't need to use force to get hold of us. He would've come of his own volition. Or are you making a practice of capturing scientists like me, the way you made German scientists prisoners after the war?"

"You too have your share of Germans working for you," Shepilov said. "The world isn't simply black and white. Nor are people all bad or all good. We all have our special interests, don't we, doctor?"

Cory walked to the door to the adjoining room, and the two

men followed him.

"If I had my way I'd open all frontiers to scientific research. Why duplicate the efforts? The world could be transformed into a paradise," Vassilov said.

Cory was aware he was genuinely distressed, but made no reply, anxious only to see Hillel.

Hillel was lying on his bed and sat up as the three men entered. Cory studied his face. His features had changed. Just as an overdose of cortisone makes people moonfaced and barbiturates which retain water in the body make people bloated-looking and benzedrine users become gaunt through loss of appetite, the RNA had added to and subtracted from Mondoro's body, chiseled off his youth, drawn lines around his mouth, etched his forehead and his cheeks.

His eyes wandered slowly from Cory to the two Russians.

"I know you," he said, staring at Shepilov, and slowly got to his feet.

"I haven't met you before," Shepilov answered. Vassilov watched Hillel, breathless with excitement. "Can you remember where you met my friend?"

Hillel's answer was unexpected. He suddenly shot forward and jumped at Shepilov, who stumbled, crashing onto a low table, which shattered under his weight. All of a sudden the room was filled with men pulling Hillel and Shepilov apart. Appalled by the outburst of violence, Cory stepped back. Three broad-shouldered men held Hillel, who struggled with a strength Cory had not know he possessed.

"You murderer!" Hillel screamed. "Murderer!"

"Hillel!" Cory shouted.

As if this was a code word, Hillel dropped his arms. His face was bleeding from a cut.

"He certainly recognized me," Shepilov said, catching his breath and getting to his feet. "That's what we wanted to know. He certainly inherited Hauser's viciousness also."

"I want all of you to leave this room," Cory said. "I want you to leave me alone with Dr. Mondoro."

"This demonstration will make history," Vassilov said enthusiastically. He could not take his eyes off Hillel's face. "I wish we could work together, Dr. Cory. I must find out how you did it."

Cory placed himself between Hillel and Shepilov.

"Get your men out of here, will you?"

Shepilov nodded to the men and left with them.

Vassilov stopped in the doorway. "Anything you want, Dr. Cory, just ask me. If I can be of any help ..."

Vassilov closed the door but remained in the room.

Hillel sank down on the bed and touched his face, looking at his bloodied hand.

"He kept mail from Hauser," Hillel said. "For years he threw away letters Hauser wrote to his wife and son. He kept Hauser's son from visiting his father. Security—that was his excuse. Hauser's brain was a treasure chest. He had to be kept in confinement...."

"Fabulous," Vassilov murmured. "Conditioned behavior. What else do you remember, Dr. Mondoro? Hauser's research? Do you think you could continue his work where he left off? Wouldn't that be a triumph for your research, Dr. Cory, if you succeeded in making one memory continue creating in another body? If inventiveness and scientific skill could be transferred?"

"Please leave us alone," Cory said. "This man is exhausted."

Vassilov opened the door reluctantly. "I don't want him to get ill," he said apologetically. "But you understand my excitement."

Cory watched him silently until he had left and closed the door.

"I'm glad you didn't talk to him," he said to Hillel, who turned his eyes to him slowly. There was no recognition in them.

Cory pulled a chair closer to the bed, "Do you recognize me?"

"Of course. I'm not blind," Hillel said savagely. He moved his head restlessly on the pillow. "That man Shepilov appeared in my dreams. How deeply are foreign engrams anchored in the memory?" Light returned to his dulled eyes. He sat up. "I'm glad you're with me, Dottore. Interesting, isn't it, how I jumped on that man. I couldn't stop myself. I'm sure Hauser would've done the same. Or was it Hauser who hit him?"

Cory watched the changeover of personalities guardedly.

"If you'd talked to Vassilov, we'd never have had a chance to get out of here."

Hillel's face softened and regained its youthful look. An expression of bewilderment came over it. "I must see Hauser's son and give him the money."

"And after that we'll go hack home."

Hillel said nothing.

"To Karen," Cory added.

"Yes. I don't know what I'd do if l didn't have her in my mind as a kind of anchor, Dottore, a hold on the life I want to return to." A look of pain came into his eyes. "After I've seen Dieter I have to—"

He stopped, turned his head away in confusion.

"You have to do what?"

"I'll know after I've seen Dieter," Hillel repeated evasively.

Hillel is still keeping secret what Hauser's memory dictates to him, Cory concluded.

Krensky had a key to the elevator. A Russian car, a Volga, built after the design of a 1952 Chevrolet, stood in front of the house. Cory and Hillel got in.

"Wallner Theater," Hillel said.

"I know," Krensky replied morosely, "but let me warn you. You can't run away to the West. Yours and Dr. Mondoro's mug shots are posted with every border guard. No use trying tricks on me. Do you think Shepilov would have permitted you to leave the house if he were not sure of security?" He turned and drove off.

Cory looked through the rear window. The street was empty except for a few pedestrians and two men on bicycles. An old woman pushing a rickety handcart harnessed to a dog cursed Krensky as he sped by too close. The blight that lay over the city brought with it a dead silence, in contrast to the bustling noises of West Berlin.

They drove in silence. Hillel's mind was obviously in a transition period. One or the other personality, Hauser's or Hillel's, would emerge, subjugating the weaker one— perhaps forever. It seemed to Cory that Hillel was in control of his actions most of the time, but that his emotions changed without warning to those of Hauser's. What was the trigger? Was there any? Or was the sudden emergence of Hauser's personality based on a biochemical change?

How could they ever get out of Eastern Germany? Vassilov had made it clear that they would never permit Hillel to leave, afraid he might reveal secrets to the West that were stored in Hauser's memory, secrets they themselves might not even know. And he could not leave Hillel. Hillel was his responsibility. Slaughter and his group might still help—how, Cory could not imagine—but they were versed in getting people across the border. There was also the State Department—after all, they were kidnapped American citizens—but their *demarche* could mean a death sentence for Hillel and himself. They might die under mysterious circumstances, and no one would be the wiser.

Cory felt a chill creep into his heart. He was a research scientist, a man with a regulated, sheltered life, a citizen who had chosen his profession. He was not a cloak-and-dagger man, he did not know how to wield a knife, how to shoot a gun, how to hide, how to break out of prison. He did not even know how to lie convincingly. He had always worked with his brain, never used physical strength except for that abortive attack on Krensky in the taxi.

Cory knew that he was going to have to fight with weapons foreign to him. There had to be a solution to this situation. He had to find it. If he considered the situation as a scientific problem, to be analyzed and examined, how would he go about solving it? This was the approach he had to take.

"Wallner Theater," Krensky announced, and stopped the car in front of a plain building. The theater was brightly lit and teeming with people. There were cars parked at the curb: Tatras, Skodas, Volgas, Wartburgs, some with Czech, Polish, or Rumanian numbers. Buses were disgorging people.

Hillel walked along purposefully; he seemed to know we to go.

"How will you recognize Hauser's son?" Cory asked.

"There he is," Hillel said. There was the warmth of recognition in his voice. Cory looked at the young man whom Hillel pointed out standing at the stage entrance, a girl at his side. He was thin, his face ascetic-looking, its skin tightly pulled over the bones, as though he was not getting enough food. The girl was loose-limbed, dark-haired. They were both talking animatedly, simultaneously, holding hands.

"Dieter," Hillel called tenderly.

At once the young man's expression changed and became suspicious and morose.

"Talking to me?"

"Yes. You're Dieter Hauser. I have a message from your mother."

The young man's face hardened. "From the Valkyrie? What does she want?"

"We'd like to talk to you," Hillel said.

Dieter looked uncertainly at the girl.

"Be nice to the two gentlemen," she said, and laughed high

and clear. She was as slim and tall as Karen and as dark. She also had the springy vivaciousness and her laughter. But Hillel did not seem to be aware of the similarity.

"What does Wotan's daughter want?" Dieter said.

"Are you working in the show tonight?" Hillel asked.

"No."

"There must be a place around here where we can talk."

"See you at the intermission." The girl smiled at Dieter and disappeared through the stage door.

"One day Eva will be a very great actress," Dieter said proudly, looking after her.

He walked between Cory and Hillel through the dimly lit Wallnerstrasse. The traffic thinned out. Krensky followed a few steps behind.

"Did you know my father?" Dieter asked.

"He's dead," Cory answered.

"I know. He defected to the West and got shot before the Amis could ship him out. The police questioned me. They know my mother too. Two traitors as parents!" He laughed dryly.

"Your father was kept in Russia against his will," Cory said. "You know that."

"That's what he told me. I didn't see him during his last years. He sent me money, though I didn't need it. I'm getting paid by the Ministry of Culture. He didn't like working for the working people. He wanted to work for the imperialists, because they pay more. And he got shot. Deservedly."

"Maybe he didn't like to work for the war industries," Cory suggested as Hillel walked on silently, obviously distressed.

"Don't hand me that lousy propaganda line," Dieter sneered. "He would have to for the Amis."

They reached a small eating place, dimly lit by electric bulbs. Krensky followed behind and sat at the next table. The small place smelled of grease and stale beer. A faded blonde was sitting behind the counter, leafing through a magazine. She looked up for a moment, then went back to her reading.

"Now tell me why my mother sent you," Dieter said, settling behind a wooden table.

"It's a complicated story," Hillel said, watching the young man's face with compassion. "Your father left money for your mother, but she refused to accept it. For her your father was a Communist, for you he's a Fascist. She told me to give the money to you."

"Well, the Valkyrie finally had a decent thought," Dieter grinned. "Hand it over!"

"It's twenty thousand West German marks, in marks and dollars and pounds."

"Foreign currency?"

"I have it right here," Hillel said, patting his pocket.

"Did you declare it at the border?"

"They didn't give me time for that."

"Beer," Dieter ordered, as the waitress came to the table. He waited until she was out of earshot.

Cory glanced at the door Two Vopos had come in. They sat down near the door.

"You must both be out of your mind," Dieter whispered. "If they catch you with undeclared West German marks and dollars, they can send you to a labor camp for twenty years."

The waitress brought them bottles and glasses, then went over to the Vopos and served them.

"Pay her," Dieter said.

Krensky got up from his table and came over to Cory. "I'd better pay."

Dieter paled; he was deadly afraid of any strange face.

"This is Krensky, our chauffeur," Cory said.

Krensky, had pulled a chair over to the table, and sat down.

"Don't worry about him," Cory said. "He knows everything and what he doesn't he finds out."

He looked at the two Vopos near the door. One was staring

at him, and Cory saw him throw back his head almost imperceptibly. Was he giving him a sign?

"My mother knew what she was doing," Dieter said. "She wants to get me in trouble. She tried to make a Nazi out of me when I lived with her. Just look around to see what good that would do. The Greater German Reich! The super race! All the women would look like her. People with dark hair would be sent to the *Leichengraben* to be shot. She is for war. I'm for peace."

Cory was in no doubt that the Vopos wanted to communicate with him behind Krensky's back. One of the men lifted his glass, pointing slightly at Krensky, the other turned his eyes meaningfully toward the street.

"Your father was for peace too." Hillel bent forward.

"That's why he tried to get out of Russia. He stayed on as long as he did because of you."

"Because of me? Don't make me laugh," Dieter said with contempt.

"He knew what would happen to you if he ran away," Hillel continued, relentlessly and with emphasis as if he were telling the story of his own life. "He was not permitted to see you for years as a punishment when he went on strike. They refused to let him write to you. When he asked to have you visit him in Baikonur, they told him he would never see you again."

"How do you know so much and how do I know you're telling the truth?"

"What reason would I have to lie?" Hillel asked. "We all hate war."

"That's strange, coming from an Ami," Dieter said. "You fight wars and make atom bombs. The overkill! Twenty tons of TNT for every man and woman and child on earth!

"When my father defected to work for you, he was killed. Now my dead father wants to corrupt me. He would have talked the way you're talking!"

"You could do a lot with that money," Cory said, quietly.

"What could he do with it here?" Krensky asked. "I could deposit it in the West in his name. That would be enough to make him independent for years. I have an account at the Hypothekenbank in Munich—"

"Now I understand. My mother wants me to return to the West, that's why she sent you to give me that story about my father. Did she say I should bring Eva?"

"She didn't mention her," Hillel said. "Does she know her?"

"Of course she does. She hates Eva because Eva is Jewish. Fortunately she wasn't born at the time of the Thousand Year Reich. That woman can't bribe me!"

"You're talking like your mother, only from the opposite side of the fence," Hillel said heatedly. "You've been brainwashed too. Bribe! Ulterior motives! You've seen nothing of the world, yet you know all the answers. The world isn't at all as it looks from the inside of your cage, my boy."

Dieter got up. At the same moment the Vopos called the waitress, finishing their beer hastily.

"It isn't as it's pictured in your brain either. I like it here. You can't conceive that anyone might want to live in a socialist country. That possibility couldn't penetrate your capitalist skull!"

He had raised his voice. The waitress and the Vopos watched him with curiosity.

"Let's get out of here," Krensky said uncomfortably. "We must get back to the pension."

He shepherded them to the exit. When Cory passed the two policemen, they signaled him.

"Leave me alone," Dieter said desperately to Hillel, who was walking at his side. "Go away, or I'll report you to the Vopos."

"Doctor," Krensky said nervously, putting one hand into his pocket. "Tell Dr. Mondoro to get off that boy's back. I don't want trouble. Let's go back to the car."

Cory disregarded him, turning to look at the Vopos behind them.

"You and your father were very good friends once," Hillel said to Dieter, walking so close that their arms touched.

"How do you know? You never met him." Dieter walked with bigger strides. He was becoming more and more frightened of the man at his elbow.

"You have a short memory. He bought you that rocking horse. You were not even an hour old when he got it for you, because he wanted to have a real horse for his son!"

"I don't remember a horse," Dieter said, eyeing Hillel's face with mounting fear.

"When you were twelve, he had you brought to Russia. He had you smuggled into the Eastern zone. He refused to work if he couldn't have you, his son. He loved you. You built that garden house together, and he made every piece of furniture in it. You liked the little house. He bought you a colt, and you loved it. You wanted to become an actor, and he forced them to send you to acting school. He spoke only German to you because he wanted you to be a German when Germany became one state again. When did you start hating him? When did they make you hate him? He was your friend and you were his only friend! He lived because you were alive!"

Hillel stopped. He did not know what he was saying; the words had welled up in him like water overflowing. But now the tide of words subsided. "Sorry—I—I'm sorry—" he stammered, and Cory knew that Hauser's memory had retreated. "I talked to you like a father would... ."

"You've never seen him and he's dead," Dieter said. A sudden panic seized him. "How can you possibly know all this? Who told you ..."

"It isn't easy to explain," Hillel answered. "I possess your father's memory. In a way, I'm your father, a reincarnation, if you want to call it that. It's the outcome of a scientific experiment."

Under the dim light of a street lamp, Dieter threw up his hands, and his body shook in fright. "That's insane!" he whispered, his face white. "Get away from me!"

"Dieter," Hillel said. "Why don't we stay together?"

Suddenly the young man turned and ran toward the theater.

"Eva!" he screamed into the dark, as if she could hear him. "Eva!"

"Dieter!" Hillel tried to follow him, but Krensky, grabbing his arm, wheeled him around.

Cory threw a glance at the two Vopos running toward him. He hit Krensky in the neck with a short chopping stroke. Krensky fell, sprawling. Cory ran, hoping Krensky would follow him, and jumped through a gaping hole in a broken wall which was supported by wooden beams. Suddenly it was very dark. Cory groped his way through the cavernous ruins of a house. He heard Krensky call the Vopos and tell them to watch Hillel.

Cory found a clearing strewn with rubble. Tall apartment houses with lighted windows stood in the distance. There were hills of broken bricks, mortar in sacks, cement-mixing machines, bulldozers. Cory climbed up a hill of serrated bricks and turned. He wanted to draw Krensky's attention away from Hillel. Krensky, a moving shadow in the dark, shouted, "Don't be foolish, Cory, come back!"

For Cory the scene was unreal: the dark sky with a sailing dim moon; the rubble covering what had once been gardens; the stillness of the night; and the small figure of Krensky, racing toward him with a gun. Behind him one of the Vopos appeared, shouting, "Let me get him!"

Krensky turned. The man reached him. Cory heard a muffled scream, then Krensky disappeared.

Quickly Cory climbed down and ran toward the spot where the Vopo knelt on the ground. Krensky was lying across a sack

of cement in a contorted position, one of his legs pulled toward his chest.

"Good work," the Vopo said to Cory. "Now get into the Volvo
with the Danish license plate opposite the beer parlor. Go on,
we haven't much time."

He started pulling the limp body over the rubble. Krensky's
head hit the broken bricks dully.

"You've killed him!" Cory exclaimed.

"I had to." The man was out of breath. "I don't want him to
be found during the next three hours."

19

Cory got into the Volvo. One of the Vopos was at the wheel. He threw his cap on the floor and put on a battered hat, then hastily took off his uniform. Underneath he wore a heavy striped woodsman's shirt. Hillel, sitting quietly in the back seat, watched with amazement.

"They're not police," he said, as Cory settled himself beside him.

"I already knew that in the beer parlor," Cory said. Those must be Slaughter's men. The atmosphere of unreality grew more and more pronounced.

Cory watched the second Vopo come running toward the Volvo and jump into the seat next to the driver, who slammed the car into gear and drove away.

"We should've moved the dead guy's car," the man beside the driver said, getting out of his green coat and throwing his cap to the floor. He too wore a heavy striped shirt.

"No time," the first one said. "We must get rid of the uniforms. They'll search the car at the border."

The second one turned to Cory with a forced grin. He was in his late forties, with a leathery complexion. "We'll be crossing into West Berlin in twenty minutes."

"Every border guard has our photos," Cory informed him. "We can't get through."

The Volvo swung into a side street, which was dark and without street lamps, and came to a rocking stop.

"Are you sure?" the driver asked.

"Krensky told me. He might've been trying to scare us."

"We can't take that chance," the second man said.

The driver started the car and swung it back into the main street.

"We have at least a couple of hours before they send out an

alarm," he said, driving on. "We can hit the *Autobahn* and be in Zinnwald in an hour and a half."

"Zinnwald?" Cory inquired.

"Yes, we'll cross into Czechoslovakia. That's the best way to get out of here. We couldn't get over any other border into West Germany; they'd certainly stop us. But there are so many tourists in the CSSR that we have a chance to disappear. The East Germans won't expect us to drive from one Communist country into another. It wouldn't make sense to them. They're a very logical people, those Germans; that's where they make most of their mistakes. You can always beat them by doing the unexpected."

"And then what?" Cory asked.

"No trouble to cross over into the CSSR with a Danish registration. They love tourists. There's an American embassy in Prague. There you'll be safe. The Amis have no representation in the Eastern zone of Germany. We're going to hit the *Autobahn* at Köningswusterhausen."

"This is the Cottbuser Damm." The second one made out a street sign. "After Karl Marx Strasse we'll start rolling!"

Tears were streaming down Hillel's cheeks. "I've failed," he said. "I couldn't convince his wife. His son turned away from him. For years he wanted to join them. He didn't expect they'd turn him down."

"But that's Hauser's life, not yours," Cory said. *"You are not Hauser."*

"That's what he wanted to do, that's what I've tried to do for him."

"All right, you've tried," Cory said, his voice hard. "Now force yourself to forget him. You are Hillel Mondoro, not Karl Hauser. The experiment is finished. Hauser is dead, and you are going back to your former life."

Hillel squinted as if he were looking into a bright light. "It's all mixed up inside me. How can I shake these thoughts?"

"Just stop worrying and leave the decisions to me. I'm not influenced by any thoughts but my own. The problem we have to solve is how to get rid of the RNA transfusion and make your mind completely Hillel Mondoro's again. In the meantime Hauser's memory has to be kept under control. I'm sure it will slowly dissipate, but there are also drugs that destroy RNA. You know them yourself."

Hillel nodded, consoled. "I know we'll manage it. When I get out of this," he said, suddenly grinning, "what material we'll have to write about!"

"It's a hundred and twenty miles to Dresden," the driver said. "Then another forty to the border. By the way, my name is Sorsen, and this is Bak. I just made up those names." He laughed. There was no mirth in his voice.

"No speed limit here," Bak said. "The little car's doing quite well."

"Did Slaughter send you?" Cory asked.

"I don't know any names," Sorsen said. "I only know that we had to trace a taxi that came from the West. We had the license number. No trouble finding it. The driver finally told us where you were staying. It took some persuasion. We knew the boardinghouse at the Friedrichs Hain. It has been used a few times before for people they want to ship out. East Germany is a Russian colony. Once here, you could well be in Russia. Same with the CSSR. Or Hungary, or Poland. When we knew where you were, the rest was easy."

"You knew Krensky?" Cory asked, intrigued at the working of the underground.

"We had his description. You told us the name, just a minute ago. His name might not be Krensky, but who cares. The less one knows, the less chance one has of getting into trouble." Bak folded both uniforms into a package and put the two caps on top of it. "At Gross Koeris we pass the Teuplizer See. It's an artificial lake. We can dump this stuff there."

"It's almost time," Sorsen said. "They'll start missing you in less than two hours. They might think that you've gone to the theater. Why not? They'll find Krensky's car and he might well be with you. When the performance is over and you don't show up, they'll blow the whistle. They might find Krensky, and they might not. I don't think they will unless they use dogs. But they wouldn't do that right away. Then the borders will be closed to you, all borders, including those to the CSSR. If we can't cross in time, we're sunk."

The car drove through the night. Dark fields stretched right and left, dim lights shone from the small farmhouses. Church steeples were painted into the light sky. The *Autobahn*, built for speed, did not pass through many inhabited places.

Cory wondered what made people accept this dangerous job. If they were stopped, the men had no chance of survival. How much money could compensate a man for risking his life by taking two people across a border? Krensky had double-crossed Slaughter for money. His chances of getting in trouble had been small, according to his arithmetic, but the margin of error had still existed and he had paid with his life. What made a man decide to hire himself out? Only the monetary reward, or was there some deeply rooted urge to play with death, to challenge the unknown, to gamble his very existence for the thrill of it? Was it the result of the peculiar workings of his body enzymes— another quirk of chemistry?

Cory decided to try and break through to Hillel's mind once more. "One day," he said, "we'll be able to separate memory RNA from other RNA's and decode it the way we determine a genetic code. Polynuclear synthesizing enzymes will be purified, and we'll learn to control the reactions to produce knowledge in the direct form of memory. Our experiment has been too broad. We transferred the bad with the good. We must be able to achieve a separation that transfers only knowledge, not the pain that goes with it."

He was rewarded by a light in Hillel's eyes that reminded him of the old burning interest when they worked together at the university laboratories.

"You'll have to start with me," Hillel said. "Where could you find a better subject? I'd like to be back at work with you. And remind me of that if I start to vacillate."

The car suddenly drove off the freeway and bumped along a side road. In the dark a body of water stretched glittering; at its far end shone the lights of a small village. Ducks quacked, alarmed by the approaching car. Sorsen stopped. Bak jumped out and ran to the edge of the lake, and dropped the uniforms and caps in the high bulrushes. He pushed them deep into the muddy water with a stick until they disappeared.

"They won't find them unless the lake gets very low, and that won't be before next summer," he said as he jumped back into the car which again headed into the *Autobahn.* He turned to Cory and Hillel. "I've got passports for you. Your names have been changed, of course. It's Frank Worthington for you"—he passed the passports to Cory—"and Cecil Taylor. You'd better learn your dates of birth and the et ceteras, just in case."

Cory opened his. His face stared at him. It was a passport photograph that had been taken five years ago. "Worthington! Taylor!" He opened Hillel's; a photograph of Hillel as a younger man, and the name Cecil Taylor, born Washington, D.C., August 8, 1939.

"American passports."

"Nothing but the best," Bak said, and laughed.

Sorsen looked into the rear-view mirror and speeded up the car. "They're after us," he muttered.

Cory turned. Half a mile away a cavalcade of automobiles sped toward them, their spotlights sweeping the *Autobahn* from side to side like a lighthouse.

"Mercedes three hundreds," Bak said. "We can't outrun them."

"Get to a side road," Sorsen suggested

"That won't help. If they're after us, they'll catch us."

"Four cars," Sorsen counted. His voice, like Bak's, was fatalistic. Cory suspected they had prepared themselves for the eventuality of being discovered and caught

"Why would they send four cars after us?" Bak asked. "They need only radio ahead."

The column sped closer.

"I might as well have told you what I know about Hauser's work," Hillel said, giving Cory an irritated look. "You'll have to spend the rest of your life in Baikonur too. They'll never believe that I haven't told you about it."

"Possibly," Cory said. "These people have a different kind of logic than we're used to."

The cars were very close now, and the lead car let out a blasting howl; lights on its roof flickered red. Sorsen swayed the Volvo perilously to the right-hand side of the road and stopped. But the column sped by.

For a few moments the four men sat exhausted and stunned. Cory had had a glimpse of a platoon of soldiers carrying automatic weapons.

"I was dead already," Sorsen muttered, starting the car and driving on.

"You might be soon," said Bak, his voice hoarse and spent.

"Government officials," Sorsen said. "Maybe the president of the zone."

"Don't call it a zone, they'll hang you for that. They aren't a zone, they believe they're an independent state, the real Germany. West Germany is just another Ami colony. Don't you agree, Doctor?" He spoke mockingly, his self-confidence returning.

"I wish it were," Sorsen said. "The whole world should be American. Then we wouldn't be afraid of being shot on an East German *Autobahn.*"

They both laughed, like men who had escaped the firing squad.

"Let's stick to the cavalcade," Sorsen said. "Maybe the border guards will believe we belong to them. Or else we can pass them."

"Not a chance. Even if we did catch up with them, you couldn't get by." Bak turned to Cory. "That car at the rear drives to the right when you drive to the right, and to the left when you want to overtake it on the left. It blocks you. It's like a dance. That's how you know one of the big chiefs is in one of the cars." He showed his teeth, uneven and crooked like tiny gravestones haphazardly pushed into the ground.

"In Prague we'll be all right," Sorsen said. "But you have to keep your mouth shut. In Prague everything is wired. The Czechs don't dare talk, even in their homes."

"Shades of Stalin. The Czechs watch everybody, but they've forgotten what they're watching for. What's to be watched? Pick up any American or Swiss or English newspaper, and you know what's going on. But they don't let any foreign papers or magazines into the country, except of course Russian ones, which nobody reads. You can't get any information."

"Superman is forbidden."

"No individuality allowed."

Both men laughed, relishing their unexpected reprieve. They had prepared themselves for death, but now it had passed them by; they gloated over their luck.

"Ottendorf-Okrilla," a sign read.

"Ten more minutes and we're in Dresden. We made good time," Sorsen said.

"The Amis bombed Prague. They were looking for Dresden, and saw a river and bridges and thought it was Dresden. They bombed Prague; just a slight mistake. I was in Dresden after the big attack. Six thousand heavy bombers. Seventy thousand bodies were heaped on the Altmarkt. Give me a clean atom bomb any day," Bak said.

Small houses lined the streets parallel to the freeway.

"I wish they'd build an *Autobahn* around this city," Sorsen reflected. "It takes time to go through Dresden. Too many traffic lights and no traffic. They like to watch who's driving through, those radishes—red outside, white inside, red-painted Nazis, those Saxons!"

The houses increased in size as the car approached the city. Rows of new apartment houses, blunt, simple, undistinguished, stretched for miles. At intervals piles of rubble could be seen heaped up behind wooden fences.

"Listen to their street names: Square of Solidarity!" Sorsen said. "Street of Liberation! But they haven't got a Street of the Seventeenth of June—that was when the East Germans revolted against their government. The only time the Germans showed guts! The Germans never had a real revolution. Things just decay, and people in a back room roll dice to pick out the new leader. The winner takes all."

"Hitler," Bak prompted.

"The Glorious Führer? That was no revolution. They loved him. He made only one mistake the Germans don't excuse. He lost the war."

Both laughed again.

"You know the Dresden motto? 'Dresden lives and works.' Look at the rubble! The whole town is still rubble," Sorsen said.

The car passed the ruins of a church. In front of it, undamaged, stood a bronze statue of a monk holding a Bible.

"That's Martin Luther," Bak said. "He started a war too. That took thirty years and almost wiped out Europe. Who won? Everybody but the Germans."

The houses became smaller again, and then the car drove along a two-lane road.

"In an hour we'll be at the border. We'll cross it or we won't,"

Sorsen said fatalistically. "The East Germans are rough with people who leave. You'll see."

Flat fields, haystacks, dimly lit houses ...

"I can't stop thinking, analyzing, examining," Hillel said suddenly.

"Analyzing what?" Cory asked.

"There's a mathematical problem that I keep dismissing from my mind, but it comes back.... Tell me, what does the symbol F usually stand for?"

"Force, free energy, focal length, capacitance—almost anything."

"In this problem F *is* expressed as a second-order partial differential with a peculiar symmetrical exponential function around zero...." Hillel made a gesture of desperation. "I can see it clearly when I close my eyes."

"Don't write anything down," Cory warned. "Not as long as you're in the eastern part of Europe."

"It haunts me," Hillel said. "If F represents magnetic force, ... between a constant Fi and the interaction ..."

Cory felt his chest freeze. What if Hauser's mind were still working on the problems he had wanted to solve before he died, problems the Russians were afraid he might turn over to the West? What if Hillel, in one of his spells, referred to Hauser's unfinished work, letting slip that the secrets the dead man harbored were still alive in Hillel's brain?

"Don't think of the formula," Cory said brusquely, "and never mention it to anyone, not even to me. Never!"

Hillel grinned. "Is it possible to stop thinking?"

"If Vassilov realizes that the transferred memory which also contains knowledge continues constructive work in its host's brain, you've locked the door forever for us to return home."

"I'm sure that idea must have occurred to him," Hillel said slyly. "Hauser had his formula worked out. He destroyed all references to it and burned all his notes. I know that, I, Hauser!"

"Just don't talk about it!"

Hillel's lips became taut. "First you try to con me into giving away what Hauser had in mind. Now you warn me not to talk or think. I don't trust you anymore."

Cory felt impotent, lost. He forced himself to try and recapture Hillel's mind.

"If you don't, you won't have anybody left."

"Hauser had nobody left," Hillel said, and turned toward the street, with its bombed-out houses, blackened walls, and signs: "Keep Out. Danger of Collapse."

And then they came to the border.

Watchtowers along the road manned by teen-age Vopos with machine guns and hand grenades. Barbed wire, man-high. A few cars parked along the road; they looked abandoned. Barracks. Large signs: "The German Democratic Republic is working for peace." A poster underneath: "Warning. High Tension."

Another barrier. Vopos with automatic rifles slung over their shoulders, looking bored. "No Photographing." Spikes pushed into the ground at short distances, at a slight angle to make cars drive slowly, obstacles like those of a ski slalom, only made of steel. "Speed five kilometers." No car could drive faster, or it would entangle itself in the spikes.

The barrier was pushed open and Vopos peered into the Volvo. Strong lights painted the road chalk-white.

"We have transit visas," Sorsen said, flashing the Danish and American passports at the border guard.

The men waved the automobile on. Cory said, relieved "That was easy."

"Just wait, there's another checkpoint half a mile down the road," Bak said, looking nervously at his watch. "That's where they might stop us, not here."

Barracks again, and a line of cars with East German license plates. Huge foreign buses. Trucks and gigantic trailers.

"We'll be held up, damn it," Sorsen said. "I hoped it'd be quiet here at night, but they seem to have closed the border, or are working with a skeleton shift. If they phoned through to Berlin…" He did not finish the sentence. His face looked ghostly in the artificial light.

The line of cars moved slowly. A guard walked up to the Volvo.

"Passports," he snapped.

"Transit to the CSSR," Sorsen showed the documents.

"Have them stamped inside, and get out of the car, all of you," the guard ordered. A stern-looking, buxom young woman in a gray-blue uniform pushed a mirror on wheels under the car, looking for contraband tied to the frame.

"I'll have-the passports stamped," Sorsen said. It sounded like a farewell.

"Is that all your luggage?" the guard asked, looking into the trunk.

"Just a couple of suitcases, not much," Bak volunteered.

"Open up. No newspapers?" The guard rummaged through the clothes.

"None."

"Leave the car here and report to Room E," the buxom female commanded.

A line of people waited at the pass control, and for the first time Cory saw the deathlike inactivity of people accustomed to waiting all their lives, standing in snakelike procession in front of stores, post-office windows, government offices, their thoughts drained out of their minds.

"Room E for foreign passports," another guard directed.

"A lot of traffic," Sorsen said, and smiled. The guard did not react.

In Room E a tired-faced man sat behind a small desk.

"Two American and two Swedish tourists," Sorsen said, putting the passports on the clerk's table. The man leafed through them. The telephone rang, and he picked it up.

"Yes," he said, suddenly staring at Sorsen and then at Cory. "License number?"

He made a note, holding the telephone receiver between his shoulder and head and shading his writing hand with his free one. Then he put a sheet of paper over the note and stared at Bak.

"Take off your sunglasses," he said. "Why do you wear them at night?"

"I have weak eyes." Slowly Bak took off the spectacles. "Don't passport pictures look as if they were taken in prison?" he laughed, but the clerk's expression did not change. He turned to Hillel.

"Your name is Taylor?"

"That's what the passport says," Sorsen replied quickly, sensing Hillel's hesitation.

"I asked him."

Hillel nodded.

"We're going to Prague," Cory said. "We're attending a symposium."

The clerk did not know what a symposium was, but the answer seemed to satisfy him and he stamped the passports. Sorsen picked them up with deliberate slowness.

They left silently.

"Let's get out of here fast," Sorsen said. They slid into the Volvo and drove off, past a barrier, where Sorsen again waved the passports, then into a hundred yards of no-man's-land and past a sign with the lettering CSSR, Czechoslovak Socialist Republic.

"We've made it," Bak whispered. "I thought it'd be the end when that East German bastard stared at me."

Another barrier. Green-clad guards stood chattering in front of a small house that had once been a farmhouse. Off the road was a tiny restaurant. Peasants carrying suitcases secured with string waited for a bus. Suddenly the world looked peaceful.

"Passports," the guard said. He had an open, friendly face. His uniform was sloppy and frayed at the cuffs.

"We don't have Czech visas," Sorsen said amicably.

"You can get one here valid for two days and you'll have to extend it in Prague," the guard said, and looked at Hillel and Cory. "Americans, huh?"

There was envy and friendliness in his voice. For him, the world ended at the border.

A rickety table stood in front of the house. Cory studied the card that the guard had put in front of him: name, place of birth, age, object of visit, duration of stay, passport number.

Uneasily he watched Hillel reading his card with a frown.

"Could I have both American passports for a moment?" Cory asked. "I need the number, so does my friend.

"B 7539," the guard read, "E 57489."

He saw Hillel hesitate.

"Dr. Cecil Taylor," Cory dictated. "Born Washington, D.C., August 8, 1939."

"Doesn't he know his own name and date of birth?" the guard asked curiously, watching Hillel. Two guards put down the beer bottles they had just opened. They too looked at Hillel.

"Of course," Cory said, and laughed. "I'm testing my memory."

The guard pushed the passports and cards through a slot in the window, which was covered by a black curtain.

"Is that the procedure?" Cory asked. "What happens in that room?"

The friendliness seemed a blind. Behind it hid the same threat of ruthless power as on the other side of the border.

"You get your visa in there," the guard said. "You'll have to pay for it in dollars." He started cleaning his nails with a large knife.

Some guards had gathered around the Volvo. "Do you have cameras? Transistor radios?" one of them asked Sorsen.

"No," Sorsen said. "Do you have a radio, Doctor?"

Hillel shook his head slowly, his face dazed and frightened. He looked like a sleepwalker. "I know Prague," he said. "I don't want to go there. It's ... like a nightmare to me."

Cory took Hillel by the arm and led him out of earshot of the guards.

"You know you've never been to Prague. Let's find a way to keep Hauser's memory apart from yours. Everything will be all right in Prague. Just don't talk to anybody until we're there."

"I wish I could describe to you the way strange pictures and situations enter my mind. Though I know that they aren't mine, they are as clear as personal experiences and have the same impact as if I had lived through them. It's like being frightened by a nightmare that persists into your waking hours. But don't worry, Dottore. I know what I'm doing, and that seems the most important aspect of this experiment. I can still control my actions."

Sorsen walked up to Cory. "If he takes long with those passports we won't get out of here." There were beads of sweat on his forehead. "The East Germans can still get us, and the Czechs can be even rougher than the Germans. They might check with Berlin if they suspect anything's wrong with the passports. Of course they're genuine, but there are always those pictures of you and your friend to give us away."

Cory glanced back at the small farmhouse. One of the large passenger buses was arriving from the Eastern zone. It carried French license plates. Luggage was piled on top of the net-covered rack.

The Czech border guard came up to Cory. "Your passports. Twenty-eight dollars for the visas."

Cory handed him the money, which the man slowly counted.

"Have fun in Prague," the guard said.

The road to Prague was clear, but they were still in a country where they could be arrested and disappear without trace.

20

The landscape changed and started to look unkempt. The houses were drab for want of paint, and the plaster had cracked, leaving large patches like open wounds. Baroque churches raised their onion-shaped domes into the night sky. The narrow, badly repaired road led through villages with unlit streets. Time had turned back to the nineteenth century. Even the factories, stabbing long, thin chimneys into the night sky, looked old-fashioned with their greasy, soot-covered windows, narrow gauge rails, and yards covered with rusty scrap iron

"We're going to deliver you to the American embassy. They'll get you out of the CSSR," Sorsen said. "And we'll be off to the country where we can take a rest. Austria."

"Hauser must've been a very depressed man," Hillel suddenly said. He had been silent for a long time. "I'm watching myself carefully, and I notice that whenever Hauser's memory emerges, I get morose. Even my vision narrows. Have you found that your vision becomes restricted when you're worried? It's as if you suddenly had blinders on, like a horse." He added to Cory's alarm.

"He was suicidal, I'm sure."

"Why do you believe that?"

"I know that he had built himself a dream world. He wanted to leave Russia and return to his wife. In his daydreams he visualized a life with her such as he'd led before the war—she was young, beautiful, the child just born. Both of course loved him. He wanted to retrace his steps. I can imagine what he would have done when he found his dreams could not be turned into reality."

"What would he have done?" Cory knew the answer, but he wanted to bring the idea into Hillel's consciousness.

"He would've killed himself."

"I'm glad you can distinguish so well between Hauser's memory and your own. You had me worried for a moment." He wished he were back with Hillel in his laboratory. There Hillel would look at this weird trip into another man's past as an adventure and not as a strand in the skein of his own personality.

They drove through a dilapidated town. The houses looked neglected and beyond repair.

"Teplice," Bak announced. He seemed to know the country well. "To think that this little town was once a lively spa—look at it now. Nobody cares if it falls apart."

"If the Amis had pumped as much money into Czechoslovakia as they did into West Berlin, this country would be thriving too," Sorsen said. "Everything on earth hinges on money. Everything. They say that happiness can't be bought. Give me the money, and just let me try!"

They had passed through Teplice.

Bak looked at the rear-view mirror. A car, a Tatra, had turned onto the road from behind a big barn. In the distance, half a mile ahead, stood a cluster of automobiles. Police were positioned across the road.

"A roadblock," Bak said worriedly. "That's new. A roadblock at night?"

The Tatra was so close that its lights shone brilliantly into the Volvo, and headlights from the roadblock bathed the Volvo's passengers in sheets of glaring white light. Sorsen stopped. At the same moment the doors were opened and the muzzles of two automatic guns stared at the four men.

"Out!" a voice shouted. Strong flashlights shone in Cory's face; he saw Hillel turn slowly, his eyes blinking painfully.

"The two in front, out!" the voice barked.

Bak made a move to get up, Sorsen raised his hands. Then the interior of the car seemed to explode. A sharp smell of cordite filled the air. Cory ducked automatically. Hands tore

Sorsen out of his seat, and he hit the road with a dull thump. Cory heard him scream. Bak slid out of sight. The glaring lights disappeared; only a flashlight shone into the car.

"Get out of the car, Dr. Cory, and you too, Dr. Mondoro," a voice said calmly.

Cory rose numbly. Still blinded, he held onto the back of the seat where Sorsen had been seconds before. He felt a slippery liquid on his palms and wiped them off.

"I was afraid you'd get hurt," the voice said, and Cory looked into the face of an officer in uniform. "Our orders are to protect you."

Sorsen was lying on the road; two soldiers pulled him across the macadam. The officer bent into the car and stared at Bak, who was lying between seat and dashboard; he seemed to have shrunk.

"He shouldn't have reached for his gun," the officer said.

"He hasn't got a gun," a voice came from the dark.

The night had become very cold. Hillel shivered.

"Please follow me to the car. The men will clean up this mess," the officer said.

Cory looked around for Sorsen, but he was surrounded by men in blue uniforms. He followed the officer automatically. The sudden attack had stunned him.

"This automobile," the officer said, and Cory stumbled into the Tatra, followed by Hillel.

The officer got in beside the driver, and the car took off. Turning on a small flashlight, the officer compared the faces of his passengers with two photographs. "You are Dr. Cory?" he asked.

"It's rather late to ask," Cory said, "after you killed two men."

The officer snapped off the light. "I hope we shall have no difficulties with either of you," he said

"The 'difficulties' the other two had?" Cory said sardonically. "Why kill those men? There was no reason. I guess since you carry guns you have to use them."

The officer did not reply.

"Where are you taking us?" Cory asked.

"To Prague."

"Good. There's an American embassy in Prague. Since I was kidnapped and taken into East Germany I've met nothing but violence. Neither of us has criminal records. We have committed no crime against the East Germans or against you. Why do we have to be dragged through such a bloody mess?"

The officer turned around to look Cory full in the face. He seemed completely without emotion.

"I couldn't say. You'll find out in time. I'm not conducting an investigation. My orders are to get you to Prague."

"I seem to meet only people who are taking orders. Nobody seems to have any authority, everybody takes orders."

"For three hundred years you've taken orders, from the Poles, the Russians, the Austrians, and the Nazis: It's become second nature to obey," Hillel suddenly burst out furiously.

"You're going to meet the people who give the orders," the officer said coldly. "Now shut up."

Cory pulled Hillel back quickly, afraid he would attack the man in the front seat.

"This man does what he's ordered to do," he said.

"That's what the Nazis said who ran concentration camps. I've heard that all my life. I'm not taking that excuse anymore." Hillel flung himself back in his corner and stared out of the window, his mouth a bitter line.

For the first time, Cory observed, Hillel had confused himself with Hauser.

Mental aggravation brought the foreign RNA to the foreground; when Hillel relaxed it receded. It was essential to keep him from becoming excited. Until he could be properly treated in a hospital with relaxing drugs, Hillel had to be kept under sedation as much as possible. Cory thought of Karen. If he could get her to come to Prague, he would have the perfect nurse for Hillel.

Driving along the road to Prague with an armed guard in front and a confused and dangerous man at his side, Cory felt lost.

In Dolni Chabry, a suburb of Prague, the Tatra stopped. The officer stepped out, and the uniformed driver was replaced by a civilian and two other men who crowded into the front seat.

"Kuçera," one of the men introduced himself, half turning around. His face was finely chiseled, and his fingers tobacco-stained from chain-smoking. The others, dressed in drab suits of coarse material, stolidly watched the road ahead.

"Why are we being kept prisoner?" Cory asked curtly.

"But you're not prisoners," Kuçera answered in faint astonishment.

"All right, then drive us to the airport in Prague and we'll take the next plane out of here."

"Sorry. I wish I could do that, but there's a slight difficulty over your unorthodox means of entering our country." His English had a carefully groomed British accent.

"How else could two kidnapped men get out of Eastern Germany?"

"That isn't for me to judge."

"Where are you taking us? To prison?"

"We've reserved rooms for you at the Hotel Ambassador in Prague. You will like its Old World charm."

"And how long do we have to enjoy that Old World charm?" Cory said, infuriated by the man's evasiveness and elaborate show of courtesy. "I suppose it has barred windows."

"Of course not. You can leave the hotel at any time. If you have never visited Prague, you can look forward to a pleasurable time. Prague is certainly the most beautiful baroque city in the world."

"We didn't run away from Berlin to go sightseeing in Prague,"

Cory said.

As an answer, Kuçera pointed out of the window. The car was passing over a big bridge spanning the Vltava River. The silhouette of the Hradcany Castle stretched filigree spikes into the transparent sky. At its feet the city was a dark wall, pin-pointed by lights.

"You will fall in love with Prague," Kuçera said softly. "It is sometimes called a second Paris, but I disagree. Prague has a charm of its own. It has no need to imitate Paris."

Cory felt a deep aversion toward this man. He felt more se-cure with the impersonal officer who had left the car. With him, the relationship between jailer and prisoner was clearly defined. But there was something sinister in Kuçera's soft, polite, friendly manner, a hidden cruelty that might show its real face at any moment.

"I want to telephone the American embassy," Cory said.

"At this time of night? There's only a watchman on duty. Besides, we have already informed your embassy," Kuçera said.

The car passed a Gothic tower which had once been part of the city wall. The street was dark and deserted except for clus-ters of people waiting at taxi stands.

Cory glanced at Hillel. He was wide awake and staring out the window as though returning to a city he knew intimately. "We're going to turn left at the next corner," he muttered, "then we'll be at the Vaclavska Namesti, the Wenzel Square with the National Museum at the end. The Ambassador Hotel is on the left. There's an alley with a movie house next door, then a department store, a cafeteria, and on the opposite side a Turk-ish bath...." He checked himself and leaned back in his seat.

"Then you know Prague," Kuçera said. "I'm sure you like our city as much as we do. When were you here?"

"I've never been to Prague before."

"You must've studied maps or photos, or talked to people who know the city well. You certainly have an excellent memory."

"How could I ever forget? The SS headquarters were in the hotel."

Kuçera looked at Hillel wonderingly. "Are you psychic? I know of a man who can tell you the addresses of people he's meeting for the first time. these things happen."

Hillel turned his face to the dark street.

"I don't accept the supernatural," Kuçera said with finality. "There's a scientific explanation for everything. Everything!" But he kept on staring at Hillel.

The Tatra swung over to the opposite side of the street and stopped at the hotel entrance. Two men stepped out of the shadow of the night and opened the car doors. Cory and Hillel got out.

"Have a good night's sleep," Kuçera said. "In the morning, I'm sure everything will be arranged to your satisfaction. These two men will show you to your rooms. Good night, gentlemen."

He signaled with his glowing cigarette and the Tatra drove off. Cory and Hillel entered the hotel lobby, flanked by the two guards.

"Rooms 331 and 332," the night clerk said. "No registration necessary. Your luggage is already in your rooms."

"Our luggage?" Cory said, taken aback. "How did our luggage get here?"

"From Berlin," the clerk said. "Didn't you send it ahead?"

When they got into the elevator, the two guards stayed behind. The elevator stopped for a moment at the second floor, where the night porter handed Cory the keys to their rooms.

Hillel laughed without pleasure.

"This is their police check. The Nazis taught these people. There's only this elevator and one staircase; everybody must pass this man. Czechs have to leave their identification papers with him when they visit anyone in the hotel." The words gushed from his lips. "In a way it's a prison without bars. The food isn't bad, the wines good, but the service is rotten; it's the same everywhere in the city. Waiters feel imposed upon; only if you tip them heavily do you get service, though accepting tips is supposed to be against the national policy. But just watch how they'll accept West German marks!" He patted the pocket where the money was hidden. "East German currency they don't take, nor rubles or zlotys. This is a socialistic country without socialists. Isn't that so, Zdenek?" He turned to the old man who ran the elevator, who had the artificially groomed look, the pronounced tiredness, of a decadent Austrian nobleman. The man lifted his washed-out, dead eyes to Hillel without a word and stopped the elevator at the next floor.

"Our rooms are at the end of the corridor," Hillel said rapidly. A very long corridor opened before them, covered with a worn faded carpet. "At this time of night you have a chance of getting warm water. In daytime the water up here stops as soon as somebody turns on a faucet. The pipes are corroded. This is Prague's number-one hotel. Kings and statesmen used to stay here ... and the SS generals. SS General Gesler had our rooms...."

"Hillel." Cory took the young man's arm and pressed it hard. "Don't lose yourself in Hauser's memory. Hauser was here, not you."

The blank look in Hillel's eyes changed to recognition. "Sorry," he said. "You're right. Gesler is supposed to be alive. If Hauser could've found him, he would've gotten even with him."

"You need sleep," Cory said. "Heuser is dead. Just remember that every time you recall his name."

"Yes, I will," Hillel said docilely.

Cory unlocked the door to his room and shepherded Hillel inside.

Hillel's face was white and drained. "It hasn't changed," he said.

The room was large, with two huge beds covered with feather-filled quilts. The windows opened onto a view of a garden restaurant far below.

Cory picked up the telephone. The night porter answered.

"I'd like to put a call through to California. Is that possible?"

"Of course," the man said. "You can talk from here to any-place in the world."

"How long will a call to Los Angeles take?"

"Not long at this time of night. The lines to Paris are free. Also those via Vienna. We can't go through Munich —that's West Germany, you know."

Cory gave the man a Los Angeles number, then hung up and shot a look at Hillel, who was standing motionless in the middle of the room.

"That's Karen's number in Brentwood."

"Yes. Yours and Karen's telephone number. Don't you want to talk to her?"

"I wish she were right here. I wish I were holding her in my arms."

21

The small apartment had become a prison for Karen. The huge bed looked abandoned. She had not slept in it since Hillel's disappearance; instead she used the Danish couch in the living room. His books and clothes, the raincoat he had worn, the shoes on the rack, his overcoat and briefcase, were like relics now that they were no longer used.

She had not left the apartment, afraid the telephone might ring.

At night she sat at the window in the dark, listening to the cars drive past the house. She had lost weight, and her youthful bounce and gaiety had been replaced by a mute apathy. She wore Hillel's cashmere pullover. Its warmth was like an embrace.

At six in the evening the telephone rang. The sound emerging from the receiver was different from that of a local call. There was a silence, and when the operator finally spoke he had a foreign accent.

Then Hillel was on the line.

She could hardly talk; her throat constricted.

"Where are you?" she cried at last.

"In Prague. Cory's with me."

Hearing Cory's name, she felt relieved. "When are you coming home?"

"Soon. As soon as possible."

"Don't leave me alone!" she cried.

"I won't," he answered, and she heard the love for her in his voice.

"What are you doing in Prague?" she asked in a sudden fury. "Tell Cory to take that awful spell off you. What has he done to you?" She couldn't fight her tears.

"I wish I could leave right now," Hillel said. "I wish I could.

But I can't.... I wish you'd come and be with me."

"I will! I will!"

His voice was gone, and Cory was on the line.

"At the moment we're detained over here," he said, and she felt the fury mount in her. "We're in no danger. None. A few things have to be cleared up before we can get out of here. There's an American embassy in Prague, and they'll arrange everything for us. Our situation is rather complex, and I can't tell you what it's all about on the phone."

His vague statements gave her a sinking feeling.

"Where are you staying? I'll come over."

"Hillel needs you," Cory said. "But check with one of the men in Washington if it's advisable for you to come."

"You can't stop me!" she shouted.

"I know. It would be better if you were here—for Hillel."

"Is he ill?" she asked in sudden fear.

"Of course not," Cory said. "We're staying at the Ambassador Hotel. If you can arrange it, come as soon as you've checked with Washington."

"I'll be there with or without their permission," she said. "I'm so happy to know where you are."

"Everything will be all right," Cory said.

Suddenly the line went dead. Karen put down the receiver and ran into the bedroom, picked up the two suitcases she had had packed for days—one with Hillel's clothes, the other with her own—and carried them to the door, as if she were leaving immediately. Then she sat down in the living room, trying to control herself. She had to be calm. She needed a passport. And a flight ticket. There was not much money in the bank account, not enough to pay for a trip to Europe. Where would she find Hillel in Prague? The Ambassador—if he was still there. But if for some reason he was not, the American embassy would know.

Borg had left his Washington number with her in case of

just such an emergency. She dialed the area code and then the secret number he had given her. She heard the cymbal of the long-distance selector, then Borg answered. She recognized his voice with its light Southern drawl.

"I had a call from my husband," she said.

"From Prague," Borg said. "He wants you to go there. I think that's an excellent idea. We'll get you a flight ticket, Mrs. Mondoro. And whatever you need. Contact TWA in Los Angeles and ask for Operator twenty-three. He'll arrange the rest."

"I need a passport."

"You'll get one in New York. One of our men will meet you at the plane. So don't worry. We'll watch out for you. Don't worry."

The repetition of those two words alarmed her. "What have you done to us? Why don't you get out of our lives and leave us alone?"

"All I can do is try to help," Borg said. "It was not our intention to involve your husband in this case. We will get him out of it. Calm down; everything will soon be all right. We have asked for a Czech visa for you. Your husband isn't in any danger."

"I've heard that from him and from Cory and now from you. Why do you repeat that he isn't in danger? I want him back."

"He's as important to us as he is to you. I'd give a lot to have him here in this country right now."

"If I have anything to do with it, you'll never talk to him again."

"Contact Operator twenty-three, TWA," Borg repeated, impervious to her bitter resentment.

She hung up. The wall of happiness that she had carefully built around her and Hillel had collapsed. She could not trust anybody, not even Cory. Nor Hillel. Nor, apparently, herself.

22

Cory had fallen asleep counting the hours he had been awake. From the night at the Hotel Europa in Copenhagen to the morning he had arrived in West Berlin to the night Krensky had been murdered, he had not closed his eyes. In his dream it seemed to him that he had not slept since he had left his apartment in Brentwood.

In spite of the depth of his sleep, he became conscious of not being alone in the room.

Opening his eyes a slit, he saw Hillel bending over him, his face a mask of hatred. The lines that lately had come to his mouth were deepened by the taut muscles of his jaw. Cory knew that if he moved Hillel would attack.

Not Hillel, Hauser. Why would Hauser want to get rid of him?

He opened his eyes and met Hillel's unblinkingly. The curtains were open and the white light of the moon illuminated half of Hillel's face, cutting a chalk-white contour.

Sitting up slowly, Cory asked, "What're you doing here? You should be asleep."

Hillel's face seemed to melt into that of the man Cory had known for years. He looked at his outstretched hands with an agonized expression.

Slowly Cory swung his legs out of bed. "Did you want to strangle me? Why?"

"I don't know what I wanted to do." Hillel shook his head in confusion and sat on the bed. "I don't even know if I thought of you when I came into the room."

Cory switched on the lights. "We must clear the issues," he said. "You're still holding Hauser's thoughts back from me."

"If only I knew ..." Hillel muttered. "New ideas strike me, new images appear in my mind. I thought perhaps you were the SS General Gesler. He occupied this room. I must've come

in here like a sleepwalker.... Gesler did something to Hauser—
I don't know what, but Hauser must've hated him.... When
will I get rid of these nightmares? How do they enter my mind?"

"Two brains in one," Cory said. "Remember how we made
experiments like this on animals, cutting their corpus callo-
sum, the major bundle of nerve fibers connecting the two cerebral hemispheres, producing a split brain? Remember how
an animal treated that way behaved essentially normally, but
a particular input given to one side of the brain was not gener-
alized to the other hemisphere, and the two cerebral hemispheres could be taught diametrically opposed reactions to the
same problem? Perhaps Hauser's RNA has stimulated only one
part of your brain. When that part is in control, you act as he
would in that situation and not as Hillel Mondoro."

"I—I knew I had to remove an obstacle. That's why I had to
come to your room.... I wasn't clear what I wanted. I was waiting for a decision which I knew would prompt me to act."

"I'm the obstacle," Cory said. "I aggravated part two of your
brain by phoning Karen and by wanting to take you back with
me, didn't I? I'm acting against Hauser's will. I am his enemy."

"I agree with you about the two spheres of consciousness,
Dottore," Hillel said soberly. "I wish I could formulate what
Hauser wanted. Then we could anticipate his moves and coun-
teract them."

"Then try to express yourself precisely."

"I always rationalize my situation and I'm perfectly aware
of what I'm doing, but the impulse of action is sometimes stron-
ger than—how can I put it—my power of observation. Your
analogy of the split brain is right. But how can I control both
parts?"

"By returning home. The familiar surroundings will sup-
press the alien influence. Train yourself to become Hillel
Mondoro again."

"Like we train animals?"

"Right. Karen will be here soon. That will be a great help to us. She carries with her part of the life you're used to."

"Yes." Hillel uttered a sound similar to laughter. "I don't think I'd have strangled you, Dottore, if that was what Hauser had in mind. I feel as if I'm under hypnosis, but one can't force someone to commit murder under hypnosis. I wonder if Hauser had murderous impulses, or if he actually killed anyone."

"We don't know that," Cory said. "But anyway, you need sleep and so do I. Why don't you sleep in the spare bed in this room?"

"Tiredness has something to do with Hauser's domination of my thinking," Hillel said, turning back the bedcover, "as though I have less resistance to his RNA when I'm tired, and more when I'm well rested."

He slid between the covers and crossed his arms behind his neck.

"Heuser must've been to Prague recently. I remember the supermarket at the corner of Vaclavska Namesti and the Graben. It can only have been there a few years."

"Go to sleep, Hillel."

"He was here during the war also. There was no movie in the alley next to the hotel at that time, and of course no supermarket. But I can still see the old German military vehicles around." He sat up in bed. "Thirty years are missing in the Czech people's brains. They talk as if the Nazis left only yesterday. They like to dwell still on the Nazi terror. It's the past to them, it can't hurt them anymore. But the present can."

"You may be talking into a microphone."

"I don't care. What they want to know they won't hear from me. How can anybody make me talk? I'm sure they had lots of trouble with Hauser. He was secretive. He didn't tell them all he discovered. He hated them. What makes them think they can get information from me? You know, evaluating our basic idea—to test RNA influence in a 'naive' body—I know now that the will can't be forced into anything if the host refuses."

He lay down again and looked around the moonlit room.

"Pandora's box," he said. "We opened it—how can we close it again?"

A moment later he was asleep.

It seemed to Cory that only minutes passed before daylight was streaming into the room. He got up quietly, showered and dressed, and left Hillel still sleeping deeply. His face was relaxed; he looked as he had during the days of their close collaboration, a time that seemed to belong to a past they could never recapture.

The long corridor was empty. No guard was posted at the door of this particular prison. His jailers knew that there was no escape. Cory walked down the stairs. The porter in his little enclosure greeted him by name.

"Mr. Kuçera is expecting you in the breakfast room, Dr. Cory," he called cheerfully.

The lobby was crowded with people and an enormous sea of suitcases. A wave of tourists had descended from a transcontinental bus which stood outside. Cory heard Dutch spoken.

"The breakfast room is up the little staircase and to the right," said a porter with a scar running from the corner of his mouth to his chin. It was easy for Cory to see that he was being watched.

As he walked into the room, Kuçera waved to him from a corner.

"Had a good sleep, Dr. Cory?"

Cory ordered breakfast and waited until the waitress had left before speaking to Kuçera.

"Do you always treat prisoners like this?"

Kuçera buttered a croissant. "Why not make things as pleasant as possible? I like to discuss problems unhurriedly and in a friendly way."

"You told me that you had informed the American embassy

that we're here."

"They knew it without us having to tell them. One can't keep secrets from them. I wish we had your American talent for organization." Kuçera looked at his wristwatch. "The American cultural attaché should be here any moment. You know him? His name is McNab. A nice fellow. But they drink too much, your representatives, if I may permit myself a criticism."

"I hope he'll bring us our plane tickets."

"To get tickets is no problem. We can always ship you out by our airline." Kuçera hesitated between different jams.

"And make a forced landing in Russia—" Cory broke off as the waitress poured his coffee.

"Russia is to the north, you're flying west," Kuçera said. "You mixed up your geography."

"What's your official title in this game, Kuçera?" Cory asked, curiously tensed by the man's casualness. "Secret police?"

"We haven't got a secret police. It died with Stalin. I'm a government official in charge of famous visitors. A kind of official greeter."

The breakfast room was filling with people and resounded with foreign voices.

"Why don't we stop this silly cat-and-mouse game?" Cory said. "What do you want? I still can see the faces of those dead men."

"Oh, there is Mr. McNab," Kuçera exclaimed and got up quickly. "This is Dr. Cory. Mr. McNab from the American embassy."

McNab, a pale-faced man in his middle thirties, looked commonplace at first glance, but then Cory noticed his shrewd eyes.

He came straight to the point. "We've sent an official request to your department of foreign affairs asking for the immediate release of Dr. Cory and Dr. Mondoro."

"Good," Kuçera said. "I'll be glad when I can wash my hands

of this case. These gentlemen are certainly not spies, and I have been left in the dark by my superiors why this affair is so complicated."

Cory turned to McNab. "When do we leave?"

"You'll need an exit visa. These people have a habit of delaying things. When will we have the answer, Kuçera?"

There seemed to be a veiled antagonism between the two men. "I'm sure Dr. Cory will enjoy his stay in Prague for a few more days," Kuçera said. "Also Dr. Mondoro, who is waiting for Mrs. Mondoro. We have just issued a visa for her. Doesn't she arrive from Los Angeles? Shall we pick her up, Mr. McNab?"

"We'll look after her," McNab said.

"She won't have any difficulty entering the CSSR," Kuçera said. "When you arrive in thc United States, they examine long lists in fat books to see if you are listed as an enemy of the country. You might be, heaven forbid, a Communist! They look through every piece of your luggage. You can't bring a fruit or a flower, not even a sandwich. That's democracy! But here you just breeze through; a stamp in your passport and you're our guest."

"And then the police get the passport," McNab said.

"Shades of the Stalin era. Habits like those aren't easily forgotten. We still have a lot of red tape. But look at all these tourists from other countries. Could they enter your country without being screened, photographed, and fingerprinted? And you talk about secret police, Dr. Cory!"

Suddenly Cory saw a face he knew. It was Wendtland, accompanied by a middle-aged dowager, fat, plumed, and jeweled. Wendtland took a table opposite Cory, and their eyes met. Cory saw no sign of recognition.

"You like to swim?" McNab asked. "There's a marvelous pool here in Prague which you should visit. It's in Podoli. Try it. Since you aren't held, have some fun."

Cory was instantly alert. These suggestions might carry information. "I love to swim," he said. "Whom do I have to ask for permission?"

"Mr. McNab just told you, nobody," Kuçera said. "You can of course leave the hotel anytime you like." He looked toward the door, which he had been watching surreptitiously for some time. "There is Professor Vassilov. You've met him, of course."

Smiling jovially, the big Russian lumbered to the table.

"How nice to see you here," he said, stretching out a huge hand. McNab introduced himself, and Vassilov lowered his heavy frame into a chair.

The breakfast room, with its Victorian design, its white bannisters painted so often that the paint had thickened the wood, its corner enclosure where a woman sat writing out the bar checks, its waiters in their old tailcoats, had the air of a past century. For Cory the room held a riptide of menace, as though the sedate atmosphere could explode into instant savagery.

"Where's Shepilov?" Kuçera asked.

"He will be here later," Vassilov said, turning his small eyes, their lids crinkled like those of a sailor who has looked too often into the sun, to Cory. "I'm extremely interested in the progress of the RNA in Dr. Mondoro."

"And Mondoro and I are only interested in getting out of here."

"That I understand," Vassilov said sympathetically. "You stumbled into it. I know it wasn't your intention; we won't hold you. But it's a different situation in Dr. Mondoro's case. You see, his memory isn't his sole property anymore. It belongs partly to us. Tell me how we can get back our share, and Dr. Mondoro will be as free as you are. Shall we do it the way King Solomon suggested—cutting the child in half and giving each mother her share?"

"I must be in a lunatic asylum." Cory was afraid of being unable to control his anger. "You can't hold him against his will. On what charge?"

"Legally they can't hold him," McNab said. "We'll have the State Department file an official complaint charging the kidnapping of American citizens and their forced detention."

Sharp as their tone was, the four men around the table kept their voices low, and the tourists in the breakfast room chattered on.

"Mondoro was not taken to the DDR forcibly," Kuçera said. "My information is that he entered East Germany of his own free will. But he crossed the border into our country under an assumed name and on a false passport, issued by you. In your country that would be a federal offense. A man would go to prison for that."

Vassilov gestured with his hands as if he had the power to smooth tidal waves.

"The case is even more complicated. It is unique in the history of science, and ordinary measures of law cannot be applied. Tell me what this means."

He took a small piece of paper from his wallet. Carefully he passed it to Cory, who saw that it was a photocopy —Vassilov had not given him the original—of a mathematical formula:

$$F = F_i + \tfrac{2}{3}f^2\{-\tfrac{1}{a}\overset{\curlyvee}{\delta} + (iK3 - \mu^3)\delta_w e^{-iwt} + (-iK - \mu^3)\delta_{-w} e^{iwt}\}$$

"I don't know what it means," he said. He passed the paper back to Vassilov, hoping he did not look as despairing as he felt.

"We found this in Dr. Mondoro's room, in the wastepaper basket. It *is* his handwriting, isn't it?"

"Well, what about it?" McNab asked, baffled.

"Dr. Hauser worked on magnetic retention of hydrogen power. This is the formula he was trying to develop." Vassilov's forehead furrowed like that of a Great Dane. "It is a much more sophisticated version of the formula we know. Symbols have been added. We can only guess what they represent.

Mondoro has solved a problem based on Hauser's unfinished research. Hauser did not publish any paper on it, but Mondoro has found what Hauser was looking for."

"I still don't know what you're after," McNab said, and looked at Cory with a blank stare.

"Vassilov is trying to suggest that Hauser's memory is still working constructively in Mondoro," Cory said. "But this is a false conclusion. Mondoro has been interested in this kind of research also. There is no proof that Hauser's RNA has anything to do with this. The formula is Mondoro's property. He found it, not Hauser."

"What would your government do if one of our people stole a secret from you that could be used against you in case of war? There is good reason to suppose that he would pay with his life."

"What do you intend to do?" McNab said sharply. "You know of course that your insinuations are too hypothetical to be considered proof."

Vassilov grinned. "We would gladly let Dr. Mondoro return with Dr. Cory if we could separate Hauser's knowledge from his."

"What a ridiculous idea," Cory exclaimed, exasperated.

"There is your answer," Vassilov said. "What is man his body or his mind? The mind is not Mondoro's, though the body is. The mind belongs to Hauser. You have no right to keep Hauser's mind."

"This is crazy, double-talk," McNab said. "We insist that Dr. Cory and Dr. Mondoro leave as soon as possible. We are going to give them asylum in the embassy until their departure. That piece of paper is no proof of anything. Mondoro is not spying. He never would have crossed this frontier if he had not been kidnapped."

"We're not holding him," Vassilov said. "The Czechs are, and it's their right since he broke their laws. You diplomats must find a solution to that problem. My recommendation as the head of the Biochemical Research Department is to retain this man. I can come to no other conclusion. Nor, I'm sure, could you in my position, Dr. Cory."

A terror like nothing he had ever experienced shot through Cory. "You shot Hauser when he wanted to leave your country. Are you going to kill Mondoro?"

"We know nothing about Hauser's death," Vassilov said. "Maybe you killed him. Why did you ship a dying man to the United States? Were you permitted to use his brain for experimentation? To operate on him was your method of extracting information from him which he might have refused to give to you."

Cory got up. "Am I permitted to leave? I can't listen to this argument any longer. To me it's completely nonsensical. I'm sure Professor Vassilov knows that as well as I."

He walked away. On his way out of the room he glanced at Wendtland, who was laughing with the woman.

Cory went down a few steps into the lobby.

A method had to be found immediately to wipe out Hauser's memory in Hillel, or Hillel would never leave this country. He would be taken to Russia and would disappear forever.

The hotel lobby, with its big red plush chairs and marble tables with Victorian legs was like a cage to Cory. He walked quickly past the reception desk, which was mobbed by tourists asking questions in half a dozen languages, and out into the street.

Everybody was carrying something, a briefcase, a small valise, a paper bag, as though hiding illegal goods.

Trying to find out if he was being followed, Cory stopped at a shop window and watched the reflection of the passing crowd. A face appeared at his shoulder, and sharp eyes met his in the mirror of the window.

"Podoli, the Plavecky Stadium." Cory did not see the man's lips move. "Take a taxi. You'll be met at the pool."

"I have no Czech money," Cory muttered, looking at a display of necklaces made of mountain crystal. But the man was already gone.

"Want to change dollars?" a voice whispered at Cory's elbow. "I'll give you thirty crowns."

Cory took out his wallet and drew out a ten-dollar bill, and felt a hand push a small wad of money into his palm.

He walked on, waited at a traffic light, turned into a side street that was fairly deserted. Again he stopped, studying some huge cut-glass vases. He felt excited by his new role. Casually he looked around, a tourist enjoying himself in a strange city.

A taxi drove by slowly and stopped as Cory hailed it.

"Podoli," he told the driver.

"Plavecky Stadium?" the driver asked. He spoke English with a New York accent, which surprised Cory. The taxi smelled dank in the rain that had started to fall.

Cory looked at the Czech bank notes depicting a Russian soldier holding a semiautomatic gun and kissing a buxom Czech peasant girl.

"You're American," the driver said. "I can tell by your clothes. I worked in New York after the war but made the mistake of returning here to visit my parents. The Czechs wouldn't let me out again. I was flying with the RAF, you know, and they didn't like that. First they sent me to the woods as a woodcutter and then they made me a taxi driver. You know what I am by profession? A pharmacist! They don't care what you know, they just push you into any job."

"Why were you sent to the woods?"

"I refused to join the Party. I'm not a Commie. But the good jobs are for Party members. Now I have to charge you one crown-eighty a kilometer, and I've to turn back one crown-thirty. What's left is for gas and for me. I'm putting in a twenty-hour day. If I didn't, I'd starve. My wife is working too, and together we don't even make forty dollars a week. The whole system isn't worth a damn. it's just one bureaucracy replacing another. Under Benes we had skilled bureaucrats, but look at them now. It's not what you know but whether you're in the Party. They don't want anybody with brains. The brains are supposed to be supplied by the chosen Party members, and only they live well. I make fourteen hundred crowns a month and I need fifteen hundred alone for food. If I don't bring home at least two thousand, we can't live. So I'm selling antiques on the side. Do you like antiques?"

"No."

"Want to change dollars? I'll give you twenty-five crowns for a dollar. The bank gives you only sixteen."

"I never do anything illegal in a country where I'm a guest," Cory said, pushing his Czech money deeper into his pocket.

"What's illegal? Everybody has a little racket or he'd starve to death. Didn't you ever hear the story of the two Americans who arrive at the airport in Prague and get an exchange of seven crowns for a dollar? Then they change more dollars and get sixteen at the bank. They have dinner and run out of crowns and change a few dollars with the waiter, who gives them thirty-two crowns, and as they walk home two of those black-market guys come up to them and offer them thirty-eight. So one of the Americans becomes frightened and says to his friend, 'I'd better phone New York. Something must've happened to the dollar!'" He laughed bitterly. "I can't get out ever, I have kids. Going swimming at Podoli?"

"I might."

"I talk too much." The driver concentrated on the traffic and speeded up the car. "But when we find a foreigner, we like to gripe. If this system here doesn't change in a hurry, the whole country is going to be one enormous poorhouse, like Poland. And we Czechs are the richest of the Communist countries!

Have you ever been to Poland or Hungary or Bulgaria or Russia? Boy, they really have nothing! They come to us, and their eyes pop out because here they can buy shoes and clothes. If this system is the future of the world, they should drop an atom bomb right now and leave the world to the insects."

The taxi drove along the river. The towers of the Hradcany Castle pointed graceful spires into the rainy sky.

"To think that this is one of the most beautiful cities in the world," the driver said. "Are you sure you don't want to change a few dollars?"

"I have enough crowns, thanks."

The driver shrugged and sighed. "I have no luck. I never had."

The taxi stopped in front of a big building with flags on the roof, surrounded by flower beds.

"This is Podoli, the Olympic stadium," the driver said, and cut off the meter. "Twenty-eight crowns, please." Cory looked into sharp, sad eyes. He paid with Czech notes and tipped the man heavily.

"Thanks," the driver said. "Shall I wait?"

"I don't know how long I'm going to stay," Cory said and entered the modern building. He paid for the use of the pool, swimming trunks, and a towel, and undressed in the locker room.

A huge pool under a transparent roof opened before him. Bleachers surrounded the long basin built for Olympic competition. Hundreds of voices echoed in the large hall.

Cory dove into the tepid water and swam for as long as he could hold his breath. As he lifted his head above the water a swimmer ran into him, and a hand pulled him up strongly. He looked into Wendtland's smiling face.

"Sorry," Wendtland shouted above the din of voices and splashing water. "I hope I didn't hurt you."

"Not at all." Cory was fighting for breath.

"Let's stay out here. We haven't got much time." Wendtland supported Cory as if helping him stay above water and put his mouth close to his ear. "They won't let you leave the country, and whatever the State Department can do will take a lot of time. They believe that Mondoro's wife is on her way to Prague and that Mondoro will wait for her. She's not coming. We'll get you out tonight."

"How?"

"You'll get instructions. Just follow them. Watch what you're saying in your room. It's bugged. See you tonight."

He dove out of sight, and a minute later Cory saw him climb out at the opposite end of the pool, and disappear, shaking his lean athletic figure to get the water out of his hair.

A group of screaming teen-agers spraying water at each other almost stampeded over Cory. Slowly he swam to the edge of the pool and sat, spent, on its tiled edge.

He had become a pawn in a game he had no desire to play but from which he could not extricate himself. It had started with his first experiment with planarian worms, then to warm-blooded animals like mice and rats, then to higher orders, like monkeys, culminating in the use of a human being.

The memory transfer, Cory realized, was only the beginning of a development that would spread into a thousand different channels. Since RNA molecules are related to viruses—molecules enclosed by a protein shell—and since viruses are parasites, they could be induced to breed. The RNA virus, carrying memory traits, could be multiplied in cultures: ideas theoretically could be bred in jars. Reduced to a powder in a hot airstream, RNA could be sprayed over a country like insecticide. Inhaled, it would enter the human system, attacking brain cells, multiplying, spreading, influencing the thinking process. What could stop a government from disseminating gaseous RNA containing selected ideas? It could not be fought by another virus, since it would occupy healthy cells. What defense could be found against such artificial contamination of the human mind?

Learning was transferable by injection. Or distribution by air. Could the human race become erudite just by breathing? Or become Fascist, Communist, peaceful or violent, at the government's whim?

The extent of this nightmare was limitless.

And, Cory concluded, if this idea occurred to him, it must also have occurred to other scientists: Russian, Or perhaps Chinese. Thousands of biochemists were working on breaking down enzymes, separating them, measuring them, trying to learn their secrets. Research was not a matter of quality alone, but also of quantity, of mutation. Somebody somewhere else would find a method of putting this idea into effect.

So far only he had been successful in transplanting RNA into a human brain and getting results. Others had failed even m minor experiments. But for how long?

As Cory walked out of the Plavecky Stadium, he saw the taxi that had brought him there still waiting for him The driver waved

"I knew you couldn't stand all those screaming kids for long," he shouted

"The Ambassador Hotel," Cory said, leaning back in the seat. Was the driver an informer? Was the man trailing him?

He felt a numb terror—and not about his present predicament, this visit to a country that was an enormous prison, nor about his personal fate, or Hillel's. The terror had its roots in the demonic possibilities of his experiment.

23

When Cory fought his way to the hotel entrance, through a crowd of people as thick as moviegoers leaving a theater, he saw the Dutch bus being loaded with passengers.

The hotel porter greeted him as if he had known him for years. At the staircase leading to the elevator the two motion-less hotel employees scrutinized the lobby for suspicious characters. A stream of German-speaking tourists clustered around the reception desk.

Only one elevator served the mob, the other had caught fire years ago and had never been repaired. It stopped at the second floor as usual, where the porter distributed the room keys, checking who was entering and leaving. Cory walked along the long corridor on the third floor to his room. A face peered from a half-open door, which closed quickly as he walked by. Fat chambermaids operated noisy vacuum cleaners on all sides. One, almost as wide as she was tall, her round peasant face smiling, waddled after Cory and followed him to his room. It had not been cleaned.

"Shall I wait outside?" Cory asked.

She did not seem to understand. She turned on the radio and connected the vacuum, which started with a roar. Suddenly she grabbed him by the arm and put her finger to her lips. Then she passed him a typewritten note and a flat key.

"The key is to the door at the end of the corridor," Cory read, while the maid pushed the vacuum through the room. "Leave at eight thirty sharp with your friend. You will be met at the bottom of the stairs. Switch on the tape recorder before you leave and place it near the radiator. Destroy note."

The maid pushed the vacuum close to the radiator, which was hidden behind a wooden screen. From under her apron she produced a small tape recorder and pushed it into Cory's coat pocket. Then she struck a match and burned the message in an ashtray. The vacuum sucked up the ashes.

Suddenly she turned and started cleaning under the bed. Cory glanced at the door. Another maid was standing there. She pulled a wagon heaped with linen into the room, measuring Cory with a shrewd look. Smiling at her, Cory peeled off one of the notes from the roll of money in his pocket.

"For both of you," he said, and left for Hillel's room.

Hillel was sitting on the bed, Kuçera and Shepilov at a small table on which stood coffee cups and a pile of petite fours. The scene was incongruously informal. Cory closed the door slowly. What had Shepilov and Kuçera talked to Hillel about during his absence? Hillel looked alert, even slightly amused, as if he were enjoying the presence of the two henchmen. His antagonism toward Shepilov had vanished. Was Hauser's memory receding?

"I explained your perilous situation to Dr. Mondoro," Shepilov said, "and he saw my point."

"Rather frightening," Hillel said. "I feel like a convict."

"Did you have a nice swim?" Kuçera asked. His smile seemed more menacing than Shepilov's frown. "The Podoli bath is unique, isn't it? I doubt if you have as beautiful a pool in the whole United States."

"I'm glad you had me watched. Something might've happened to me in this strange city."

"This is a city where everybody can wander about without danger. Even women, on side streets and after midnight. I understand that no woman would dare to walk alone after dark in one of your cities. But we couldn't let you roam around without knowing where you were. Mr. McNab suggested that swim to you; I wonder why. But we might be too suspicious."

"What can you offer for tonight? A concert at the Klementinum?"

"I think it's better that you stay in," Shepilov said "Our men don't like to work at night. But we wondered where you got the money to pay for the taxi and the swim. You had no Czech money with you and didn't change any here at the hotel or the bank."

"I bought the crowns on the black market," Cory said "Three hundred for ten dollars."

"The black market is against the law," Kuçera said.

"You have so many charges against us, I doubt if a new crime will make any difference."

Cory felt the muscles of his shoulders and arms tense an awareness he had experienced before only when a laboratory test suddenly promised exciting results.

"You have accumulated a great number of serious offenses," Shepilov said sternly. "You could be sent to prison for life."

"I never wanted to be here in the first place," Cory answered. "All those so-called crimes were forced on me by circumstances you created, not I."

He looked around the spacious, old-fashioned hotel room with its large beds, ample closets, windows opening onto a cluttered maze of roofs with the graceful towers of the Church of the Lady of Tyn rising above them.

"Is this to be our prison, or are there others, better ones?" he asked. "I've heard about the dreadful Communist prisons, and I can tell them at home that it's not the case. Your prisons even have room service."

Shepilov looked at him, and his eyes glittered like metal. "I realize you're the victim of a plot hatched by the CIA and that you were forced into committing crimes. We know that Dr. Mondoro was anxious to visit East Berlin but was stopped by that nefarious organization."

"Your information isn't quite correct," Cory said. "You forgot to tell us why we were driven across the East German border against our will."

"Dr. Mondoro assured us that he paid the driver to take him there," Kuçera said. "You were not kidnapped."

Cory looked at Hillel. "You told them that?"

"Kuçera said it, not I, but I didn't contradict him. I just listened. I wanted to go to East Berlin, didn't I?" Hillel turned sharply to Shepilov. "But why were we kept prisoners in East Berlin?"

Shepilov dismissed the question with a wide gesture. "What gives you that idea? You even went to the Wallner Theater to see a Brecht performance that night. You changed your mind." Shepilov filled his cup with coffee as he threw the accusation quietly at Cory—"and instead you helped a couple of CIA agents to commit murder:"

Cory tightened his lips, determined not to reply.

"After that you drove through the DDR and crossed into Czechoslovakia, using a forged passport which the two agents gave you. That indicates that the murder was premeditated," Kuçera said. "The border police wired your and Mr. Mondoro's passport pictures to Prague, and we checked with our friends in Berlin. They asked us to arrest you and the two men. Unfortunately the agents attacked our police and had to be shot in self-defense. I'm sure your State Department will shift the blame onto us in the usual way. But we have proof that you are both guilty of crimes against the security of the DDR and the CSSR. We might have to send you back to the DDR for punishment, should that independent country ask for you."

"If we applied your kind of so-called logic to our scientific research," Hillel said, with a lucidity that convinced Cory that he was free, for the moment, of Hauser's memory, "we'd still be back in the stone age."

Shepilov sighed. "I pleaded your cause with Mr. Kuçera, who feels sympathetic toward you. So far there is nothing in the files about you. Mr. Kuçera has deliberately refrained from making a report. If you ask your government not to interfere, we might be able to help you."

"Help us?" Cory asked.

"Yes. I would invite Dr. Cory to lecture at the university in Moscow about his research in RNA and maybe conduct some experiments with Professor Vassilov, since Dr. Cory, as I understand, has not published his latest findings. Since Dr. Mondoro assisted Dr. Cory, he also would be of value. Mr. Kuçera would permit you both to leave the CSSR to visit the USSR. Once there, you would be outside Czech jurisdiction, and I don't believe the DDR would ask for your extradition."

"And we could leave Moscow anytime we wanted," Cory said. "This is what you had in mind all the time, of course."

"How could we hold you?" Shepilov asked. "There is no case against you within our borders. Though I don't know what Professor Vassilov's decision would be in your case, Dr. Mondoro. That is not for me to decide."

"There is no rush," Kuçera said, helping himself to a piece of cake. "We have issued a visa for Mrs. Mondoro. She has booked a flight to London and will take the Czechoslovakian airline to Prague tomorrow afternoon. She will be in Prague at seven twenty in the evening. Dr. Mondoro might like to take her to Moscow."

"Then she's a hostage." Now Cory understood Wendtland's decision not to send Karen to Prague.

"There is no reason to use such words," Kuçera said. He sounded annoyed. "All we want is your cooperation."

"You've worked everything out very well," Cory said, acting out his part in the farce. "We leave for Moscow the day after tomorrow with Mrs. Mondoro. is that your plea?"

"It's only a two-and-a-half-hour flight from Prague," Shepilov said.

"This room," Hillel said, getting up, "wasn't it occupied by General Gesler, the head of the SS?"

"Yes," Kuçera said, surprised. "And we believe that he's still alive."

"Nobody saw him die." Shepilov looked at Hillel as if he had the answer.

Instead Hillel said: "We're confined to our rooms. Why?"

"There is room service. Order whatever you like, be our guest," Kuçera said easily. "But we would prefer you stay here until your wife arrives."

"We have no place to go," Cory said. "You Slavs are good chess players. Your moves have been very well planned."

"I love a good game of chess," Kuçera said. "I'll take you on anytime, Dr. Cory."

"Anytime." And Cory wondered how much they knew of Wendtland's plan.

Cory waited until the waiter had rolled the serving tray out of the room and closed the door. Then he quickly wrote an a piece of paper, "Karen is not coming. We're going to be helped to get out of here." He pushed the message across to Hillel. The food Cory had ordered had taken a long time to arrive; the time to leave was close at hand. Watching the waiter lay the table seemed to take hours. All the while he kept up a conversation with Hillel, knowing they were being listened to and that the waiter was probably an informer. Cory had guessed where the microphone was hidden; the maid had pushed the vacuum cleaner deliberately close to the radiator.

"I like their Plzen beer," Cory said aloud toward the radia-tor. "I like the bitter taste of the hops."

Having read Cory's note, Hillel tore it slowly into shreds, and, as though performing some ritual, dropped it into the ashtray and set it afire. If he was concerned about the mes-sage, he didn't show it. Cory had the impression that Hillel, too, was anxious to terminate his involuntary visit to Prague. Cory pointed to his watch and to the door.

Hillel nodded, and went on with the story he had started when the waiter was serving the food. "Gesler wanted to get information from Hauser right here in this room. He was told by the SS that Hauser was suspected of having taken part in the anti-Hitler plot of 1944. Hauser and Gesler had met in Peenemunde. He was there when it was bombed. Remember my dream, Dottore?"

"Yes." Cory went to the bathroom and hastily pocketed his toothbrush and electric razor, just to have something to do. The order was to leave at eight thirty; from there Wendtland would have to take over. What would he do if there was a guard in the corridor? Attack him? The idea was absurd. He was helpless when it came to violence.

Hillel kept on talking. "When the German Gauleiter Heidrich was murdered by Czech paratroopers dropped by the British, Gesler had thousands of Czechs shot. It was completely indiscriminate. Once he had every man arrested in the post office on Opletalova Street, just around the corner from this hotel. The men were taken to the yard where the mail trucks were parked and machine-gunned. Imagine, unsuspecting people buying stamps and mailing letters ending up against a wall and being murdered! All on Gesler's orders."

Hillel poured coffee on the cinders in the ashtray and ground them down with a spoon. Cory returned from the bathroom, feeling foolish. His and Hillel's lives were at stake and he had thought of taking along his razor! He met Hillel's eyes, sharp, wide awake.

"Where's the microphone?" he wrote on a piece of paper, and showed it to Hillel, who started to move in a silent search along the wall.

"Hauser must've hated Gesler," Cory said.

Six minutes to go.

"I wonder if there's a guard outside our door," he wrote.

Hillel had found the microphone's outlet, a small hole in the wall behind the radiator. The wallpaper around it had been tampered with. Hillel pointed.

"We're being listened to all the time," he said, deliberately raising his voice a little. "That's one way of saving guards. I wonder if they have microphones in every room."

"Kuçera's way of playing chess," Cory said. He produced the small battery-operated tape recorder and placed it close to the radiator. "Kuçera believes Gesler's alive," he said, to keep on talking.

"They also think Bormann's alive too. There're plenty of people who know where they're hiding and under what names. Hauser once received a mysterious message in Baikonur from one of the captured Germans working for the Russians. The man believed he knew where Gesler was living. If Hauser knew, he didn't tell anybody." At the very moment of escape Hillel was still tormented by Hauser's memory.

Cory looked at his watch. It was eight twenty-nine, time to leave. He switched on the tape recorder and walked to the door. Hillel's voice came clearly from the loudspeaker.

"I'm in full control of my will. I had one shock, that was when I left for Copenhagen. There are moments that I can't remember...."

Hillel's voice trailed on. Hillel listened for a moment, startled, then quickly followed Cory.

So Slaughter had recorded their conversations in Copenhagen, Cory thought. There was nowhere you could hide from the spies; they had instruments that could listen through walls.

"What actions?" Cory's voice came from the loudspeaker.

"Desires anchored in his past," the recorder continued, "which now would come to the fore...."

Cory peered outside. The corridor was empty. He crossed it quickly. Hillel closed the door behind him. The voices still continued inside Cory's room for the benefit of the invisible guard.

The key fitted the door at the end of the corridor. It screeched on its hinges. Both men stepped onto a small landing. They closed the door and locked it. In the dark, Cory's hand slid along the rail. He felt Hillel's breath on the nape of his neck.

Voices and the clatter of dishes came from below. As their eyes adjusted themselves to the darkness, they could faintly make out the stairs, partly blocked by discarded furniture, bales of old newspapers, buckets, worn-out brooms. Apparently the hotel never threw away anything. Hillel stumbled. For a minute both men stopped, holding their breath. The voices ceased; so did the clatter of dishes. The hotel seemed to listen with a thousand ears. Only the orchestra down in the basement kept on playing.

When the voices resumed, Cory continued groping his way through the dark, which became deeper the farther he went. Like a blind man he anticipated obstacles. The steps finally came to an end, and light fell dimly through dusty transoms. The door leading outside was locked; its rusted handle had not been disturbed in years. A truck drew up outside, garbage cans clattered loudly, and voices could be heard.

The garbage truck moved off. Suddenly the door swung open. The hotel's service yard was cluttered with empty garbage cans. Lights shone from hotel windows above. Below the orchestra could be heard playing a waltz.

A small rickety baker's truck backed into the yard, its back door swinging open.

"Hurry!" a voice came from within. Hillel jumped inside, Cory scrambled after him, the door closed, and the truck's gears meshed noisily as it drove off. Cory found himself in complete darkness. He heard a man breathing close by. The air smelled of stale bread and exhaust fumes.

"You left the recorder on, I hope." The voice had a refined British-German accent. Wendtland's!

"Of course I did," Cory said.

"We have another hour; that's how long the recorder will run. I trust you had the dishes removed by the waiter. He may return and report you missing."

"I didn't have time," Cory said. "The food came up so long

after I'd ordered it, I didn't dare call the waiter again."

"Bad mistake," Wendtland said. "Now I don't know if we still have that hour. I had to splice together lots of your dialogue. I used every scrap of tape, every inch I could find, even when it didn't have continuity or sense."

"You must have recorded us as far back as California," Hillel said.

"We had listening devices in the apartments next to Dr. Cory's and yours. Yours we couldn't use, since there was that woman's voice in it."

"Karen," Hillel said. He spoke the name deliberately and for the first time since he had left California. "Why did you check on us?"

"We couldn't take any chances."

"But you took them coming to the CSSR," Cory said.

"Slaughter wouldn't do it, though it was his job. He said with my German accent it wasn't such a great risk traveling with a group of Dutch tourists. Now I begin to wonder. They must be looking for me. I didn't leave with the group. One always leaves traces behind, unavoidably, One can only hope that those who watch you can't break the code."

"How can we get over the border in this truck?" Hillel's voice came from the dark.

"We'll fly out. We've got a plane. The plane has clearance to leave the CSSR. It's a four-seater, a Czech plane, a replica of the American *Apache*. We bought it with money we got from the whale."

"The whale? What whale?"

From the darkness, Cory and Hillel could hear Wendtland sigh.

"I don't expect you to believe me, but there's this stuffed whale that travels through Europe in a trailer a hundred feet long. The whale of course is old; I remember having seen it myself when I was a child. But doused with formaldehyde daily, it has remained preserved. And it's taken from one town to another so the people can come see it. You wouldn't believe how many want to look at the whale; it has been seen by literally millions of people. And the daily intake is fantastic—about thirty thousand crowns, more than three thousand dollars! It made about two hundred thousand crowns in Poprad alone, a small town on the Polish border. With the money the owner buys anything that can be shipped abroad and sold—horses, hunting rifles, glass, anything. This time we bought a plane." He laughed quietly. "It will be the end of the whale if they find out."

"A whale!" Hillel sounded as if Wendtland had lost his mind.

"I told you you wouldn't believe—"

The truck swerved severely to the right and came to an abrupt halt. Wendtland pushed open the door, and Cory found himself behind a small farmhouse. A large meadow stretched toward a pine forest; a row of new apartment buildings lined the horizon. Waiting for them was a Skoda with its engine running and a man sitting impassively behind the wheel.

"You too play chess," Cory said.

Wendtland did not understand. "Get inside," he said, without taking any notice of the driver. "We should be in Ruda in ten minutes. The plane will pick us up there."

The country road was deserted.

"If they shipped you to Russia we'd never get you out. The Russians aren't as lax as the Czechs," Wendtland said. "The Czechs don't like Russians, they like only Czechs."

"We haven't left yet," Cory said. He looked out of the rear window, expecting a cavalcade of cars to come chasing after the Skoda. Past and present mixed in his mind. Here he was in a car again, apparently driving to safety. But any moment a roadblock might loom up. Was it hours or days ago that he was driving with Hillel and two people lay in the dirt?

"We really wanted to take you to the American embassy, but

we were afraid you'd never leave without being arrested. So we decided to do it this way."

"I don't know how I got mixed up in this," Cory said. "I belong in the lab at the university, not in a Czech car driving someplace I've never even heard of."

Wendtland lit a cigarette. "If your friend hadn't flown to Copenhagen, we wouldn't be on a Czech country road now. Blame him for giving us a good chance of getting shot. You joined a war. You didn't volunteer; you weren't drafted. You just drifted into it. For me the war has never ended. It never will. It's part of my life."

"Maybe you enjoy danger," Hillel said. He had been quiet since they had left the hotel. *"Kein schonren Tod gibts auf der Welt als wer vom Feind erschlagen."*

His German accent was perfect. Wendtland looked at him curiously. "No death more beautiful than being killed by the enemy," he translated. "Where did you learn your German?"

"By a very unorthodox method and extremely fast," Hillel said, and grinned. "But I wouldn't recommend it."

Wendtland looked sharply at him; his Prussian-blue eyes glittered.

"I finally get some positive information from Dr. Mondoro. You can't deny anymore that your methods showed positive results, Cory."

"That Mondoro can utter a few sentences in accent-free German is no proof of anything," Cory said. "Any parrot can do that. The more you delve into science, Wendtland, the more confused you become. The only certainty is that there is no absolute proof of anything."

"Suit yourself, Cory." But Wendtland was smiling.

The car drove onto a dirt road and came to a stop. Wendtland quickly got out, looked about him, and knocked on the window, beckoning them to follow. Sheltered by a cluster of birch trees, they stood silently. A bright moon broke through and seemed to race along the sky. Then the faint sound of propellers purred from the low-hanging rain clouds.

The driver turned on the car's headlights and illuminated the meadow before them. He drove, bouncing over the uneven ground, guiding the plane down. It hit the grass with wings tipping precariously and propellers feathering. Wendtland ran toward it with surprising speed.

The Skoda turned off its lights and disappeared along the country road. A few minutes later the pilot gunned the plane and took off with his three passengers, climbing steeply until the windows were covered with a gray haze of protecting clouds.

The green lights of the dashboard deepened the fissures in the pilot's gaunt face. To Cory he looked like Bak's brother. They seemed to be a special breed who would risk their lives for a cause known only to them. A voice came over the radio. The pilot picked up the microphone and spoke in Czech.

"They want to know why we dropped our altitude," he said in accented English. "Prague is watching us on radar. We need twenty minutes from here to the West German border. I told Prague that I had to fly very low to find out where I was."

The world below Cory was dark, punctuated by lights from small villages. A few car lights crept along invisible roads.

"We're ordered to follow the flight path that Prague has laid out for us and pass over Plzen. There's a military field. I'm sure we'll get company," the pilot said.

Again the radio chattered.

"They want us to land in Plzen," he said. "I told them I would."

"If we land we're through," Wendtland said.

"If we don't we'll be through also," the pilot said. He set the throttle at maximum speed. "If we can hold them till we've passed Plzen, I might make the last forty miles to the border in ten minutes. If they send up jets, they'll force us down."

Cory looked around the small cabin, at Hillel, withdrawn

and silent; at Wendtland's masklike face: the gaunt features, the high cheekbones, the dueling scars.

"Would they follow us into Germany?" he asked.

"They wouldn't dare ... I hope," the pilot said. "Though they can always pretend they hit us in the CSSR and we crashed across the border. Who could prove it?" He pointed to a cluster of diffused lights and a bright band of a landing strip. "Plzen," he said. "From here on we can only pray."

The plane began to climb.

"I was told to fly at fifteen hundred feet. If I can keep in the clouds, we have a chance."

The radio began to call again. The pilot answered.

"I told them that I have to circle before landing. That will give us another minute or two."

Clouds wrapped the plane in a blind. The radio barked orders.

"Tell them you can't see the airfield," Wendtland said. "That you've lost your bearing."

"I did that. I'd better keep on talking."

"If you can keep talking for another ten minutes, we're across."

"How I love those clouds." The pilot's voice was hoarse. "One of their planes has us on radar. He radioed that he has orders to shoot us down if we don't land."

"Drop way down," Wendtland ordered. "Fly over houses. Maybe he won't dare use his guns."

The pilot pushed the stick forward, and the small plane went into a steep dive. The ground came up rapidly. Cory saw a church steeple; the lightning rod on its tower looked as if it were going to pierce the plane's belly, and he could see a large nest on the roof with three storks in it. The storks looked up, and the largest one spread its wings protectively. Cory peered through the window.

The fighter plane was diving at them.

Treetops raced beneath them, small tile-covered roofs, tiny gardens, clusters of cattle. Cory searched for the jet. It had pulled out of its dive and shot skyward in a sharp arc. It turned.

"We're finished," the pilot said hoarsely. "That MiG will open up on us."

"Go still lower," Wendtland ordered, his voice brittle. "There's a bunch of people down there at the church square. Buzz them. The MiG won't dare shoot."

The pilot went into a low dive; quickly the ground came close. They were now lower than the church steeple.

"Feather the propeller," Wendtland shouted.

The darkness of the night was suddenly shattered by the glaring light of a magnesium flare, which slowly parachuted to the ground. Cory saw startled white faces staring up at him. He heard the swoosh of the jet. The people below scattered; some threw themselves on the ground.

The pilot gunned the plane, just lifting it over black treetops. The jet had pulled up sharply into the sky, preparing for another pass.

"Why didn't he shoot in spite of the crowd? His orders were to get the plane," Wendtland said disbelievingly. "I would have followed orders."

"Glad you're not the pilot," Hillel said.

It was night again, deeper now that the flare had burned out. Suddenly from the ground two sharp lights penciled into the sky, searching for the MiG.

"The border! The border!" the pilot shouted. He tipped his wings up, precariously close to power lines. A low barbed-wire fence was strung unendingly along a ditch in which sluggish water flowed. The light beams concentrated a moment blindly on the plane's cabin, became extinct.

"We're over," the pilot said.

The plane slowly started to climb. The MiG had disappeared. Too exhausted to talk, Cory stared into the night.

Wendtland lit a cigarette, his hands steady. "I've been through moments like this before," he said, unmoved. "'If you never risk your life, you'll never realize its sweetness!'" he recited. "That's a quotation from a German poet." He pulled on his cigarette. "Funny, since becoming an American citizen that line doesn't make much sense to me anymore. I'm afraid I've lost my German zest for dying."

24

Content with himself, Slaughter walked down Bahnhofstrasse in Zurich. Half an hour ago he had received a message from his contact man in Germany that the Czech airplane had crossed the border safely and would be in Switzerland within an hour. Slaughter had immediately arranged a landing permit at the airport in Dubendorf. Karen Mondoro had arrived the night before from New York and had been installed in a double room at the Carlton, a small but comfortable hotel on the Bahnhofstrasse. He had also reserved rooms for Cory and Wendtland. In the morning an American jet would fly them to New York. Washington would be the next stop.

Once in Washington, the pursuit of a man charged with a chemical called RNA would be over. Whatever secret he divulged was not Slaughter's concern. Experts would be assigned to the case. Cory would be sent back to the university, thus ending his damaging interference. But the glory of having brought Mondoro back to Washington would be Slaughter's. There would be a promotion, maybe even an important assignment abroad. He wouldn't mind having his headquarters in Zurich. He liked the pretty city with its comfortable restaurants, its bridges over the Limmat River, its staid citizens, not unlike those of clannish and aloof Boston. The stores that lined the Bahnhofstrasse displayed goods as fashionable as those of Fifth Avenue and Bond Street. Well-groomed women, Swiss and foreign, filled the coffee houses and hotel bars.

Slaughter ordered a cup of coffee at Huguenin's and a Baseler Kirsch, a rather potent drink whose pungent flavor he had learned to like, and did some girl-watching before leaving for Dubendorf to meet the plane.

He doubted that the Czech government would protest the unauthorized removal of two people by plane. What grounds would they have? There was no official report of Cory's and Mondoro's crossing the border on false passports. The Russians and East Germans would be furious; Slaughter dwelled lovingly on the prospect. He had beaten them in the game at which they believed themselves masters. Krensky had paid with his life for his deceit. The Czechs hadn't gained anything by picking up the two agents; they had died before they could be made to talk.

Slaughter picked up his new English hat and umbrella, which he had bought at Keller's, and hailed a taxi to Dubendorf Airport.

Air France, BEA, Alitalia, SAS planes rolled in and took off, a microcosm of the unified Western world, a world he was protecting from the-inroads of Communism.

The plane came in earlier than he had anticipated. The three passengers looked strained. Slaughter enjoyed the displeasure in Cory's eyes at the sight of him; he disliked Cory's independence and disrespect for the authority he represented. It started to rain. Slaughter put up his umbrella. But I've got you where I want you now, Cory, he thought; you'll be running the way we want you to.

"I need some sleep," Wendtland said. He looked thinner and pale. "So do Dr. Cory and Dr. Mondoro."

"Mrs. Mondoro is in Zurich. I made a special effort to get her here in time. We never intended to send her to Prague, Dr. Mondoro," Slaughter said. "It was a ruse to get the Czech visa for her. I wanted the Czechs to believe that you were waiting for her. It worked."

Cory watched Hillel's face. It was unemotional. Was he happy to meet Karen? If he was, he didn't show it.

For Cory the adventure had ended and work had begun, planning to eliminate the foreign RNA from Hillel's brain. They had discussed the subject together and Hillel, very lucidly, had added his ideas. Minnie the chimpanzee would be used for the tests. If enzymes succeeded in eradicating the RNA she had got from Oscar, her mate. the same Procedure might be tried on Hillel.

Enzyme ribonuclease, which the Russians used for their experiments, might be employed successfully. Cory was optimistic.

But during the discussion Cory had had the impression that Hillel had other things on his mind. His cheerfulness was artificial; he seemed to be forcing himself to look unconcerned.

Driving into Zurich, Cory felt the gray curtain lift, the depression he had experienced behind the barbed wire of East Germany and Czechoslovakia. The houses the taxi passed looked cleaner than he had seen in days.

"You're going to see your wife in a few minutes," Wendtland said. No one will disturb you until we fly out of here, Doctor."

Hillel looked relaxed to Cory, his tension gone. The danger had passed once he had moved into the world of reasonable and predictable people again.

"If you want a nice cozy dinner, I'd like to take you to a restaurant at the Limmatquai," Slaughter said. "You get venison there, and it's delicious. You can't have venison in the States, it's against the law. Our hunters would shoot all the deer and serve them as deerburgers." He showed his long polished teeth.

From the smell of cordite and blood to small talk, Cory thought, all within a few hours. Death in this city of burghers only happened in bed.

"This is the Hauptbahnhof, the central railway station." Slaughter played the guide. "Your hotel is farther up this street."

"I know," Hillel said. "I studied mathematics here in Zurich. I know the town well."

Cory stiffened. Hillel had gone to UCLA. The parts now seemed to be reversed: it was Hauser who sat beside him, hiding behind Hillel's facade, determined to carry out plans he was keeping secret, plans that might wreck Cory's hopes for the future of Hillel Mondoro.

"There's no earthly reason you should have come here to pick me up like a child that can't travel alone," Hillel said. "Wouldn't I have told you to come if I'd wanted you to?"

"You did," she said. "You phoned me. Have you forgotten?"

He was standing near the door, staring at her, trying to remember. Then he shook his head. "That isn't true."

Her face drained of blood, Karen watched him with unconcealed horror. This was Hillel who looked at her, his face, his shape and form. But his being, the man she loved, had been replaced by something alien. Cory had told her that Hillel would be able to shed Hauser's memory. But could he?

Waiting for him in the hotel room in this strange city, far from home, suddenly she had been beset by a fear that echoed the days of loneliness in her apartment, the scrambled maze of happenings to which she could find no logic.

When Hillel came in, she had run up to him and embraced him. They had stood for minutes, holding each other without talking. The unhappiness, which she had felt, was still there, and she had tried to find relief in his arms.

"We're going back tomorrow," he had said. "I won't leave this room until we both leave together."

This was the assurance she needed. She had kissed him, and in the response of his kiss she felt the deeply rooted fear that possessed him.

They had had dinner in their room. They had talked, not about him or the future, but about the past when they first met. They had laughed about small incidents that had cemented their love for each other, hoping to give their new life stability: the time he took her out and ran out of money, and had to leave their driver's licenses with the waiter; the morning he picked her up for a short stroll, and they talked and talked, until they found themselves miles away from her apartment; the day she made up an excuse to drop by his room, driven by the need to be close to him (they did not leave his room for two days).

The night in the hotel room in Zurich had reminded her of that first burning love. Hillel was holding her again, but not with the love of six years ago; it was a love consumed by fear. He was afraid of himself and trying to find strength in her.

Then in the morning, before daylight, he had suddenly torn himself away from her and sat up in bed. As her hand touched him he cried, "Don't come near me."

Shocked, she had watched him disappear into the bath room, picking up his clothes on the way. She dressed hurriedly, as if that would give her some protection. He reappeared, shaved, and picked up his coat, a stranger who looked at her with sudden hatred.

"What's the matter?" she had asked.

"I have to leave. I should not be here."

Then she had known she had lost him, that his love of the past night had been a vain search to find himself again. Now he stood there before her, sullen, mistrustful, even denying that he had telephoned and asked her to come to him.

"I can't reach you," she said. "How can I make myself clear to you? It's not you who's talking to me."

"I know what I'm doing," Hillel said. "Better than ever before."

"If you could only listen to your voice, you'd know you're sick, desperately sick," Karen said. "You must force yourself to disbelieve your impulses. Cory told me that you'll recover. Why don't you believe in him even if you can't believe in me?"

Her words seemed to penetrate. "If you could only wait," he said, "everything would be as it was before."

"Wait for what?"

"I have things to do, to get rid of this ... compulsion. It is a compulsion, Karen. I know it is, but I can't shake it. I have to do one thing more, and then I'll be free."

She retreated to the window, and he took a few steps toward her.

"I never knew what it meant to be forced to do things. I always believed that I was in full control of my will. But sometimes you have to act, even if you don't want to. I'm like an addict who can find relief only by taking dope. I've never taken a drug, but that's what it would be like, I guess. I can't stay here either. I have to go on. To do this one thing more! I must!"

Karen felt a wave of pity, but could not make herself go closer to him. If he were the Hillel she knew, she would be at his side, embracing him, consoling him. She might even be able to persuade him to stay with her. But that weird strangeness between them kept her away.

"I—I couldn't even be with you," Hillel said, forgetting the night passed. "I know I couldn't. They mutilated Hauser."

"That was Hauser. You are Hillel Mondoro. Just an hour ago—"

"I don't know," he said. "I don't know who I am."

Forcing herself to overcome her terror, she stepped forward.

"Don't touch me," he said.

She stopped. He was a madman. She had to get advice and help from Cory. She did not know how to fight this thing, which was as elusive as a ghost and just as inexplicable.

An idea struck her that was possibly the key to his strange and sudden abhorrence of her. "Hauser was a German brought up under the Nazis. I'm Jewish. Is that what makes you suddenly withdraw from me?"

He stared at her, an indefinable smile on his lips.

"So are you," she said harshly, "Jewish. Hillel Mondoro, whose grandfather was a rabbi."

"Why bring that up?"

She came closer, her eyes wide. "I wish I could pray. Why wasn't I taught to pray? You went to the synagogue on High

Holidays, you know how…remember?"

The words seemed to soothe him. "If I could only sleep," he muttered. "Sleep always helps. I can think better afterward. This stuff has less effect on me when I'm rested."

He threw himself on the bed and closed his eyes. Karen hurried over to Cory's room. He had not gone to bed. He was sitting by the window.

"How did it go?" he asked. She sensed he knew the answer. "What shall we do?"

She sat down, her arms heavy in her lap, her boyish body ramrod straight.

"He told me that he has 'things to do.' Does that mean he's going to run away again? Where is he running to, Dottore, what makes him run? What does he want? When he is Hauser, he's even anti-Semitic. He hates me because I'm Jewish."

"Extraordinary!" Cory said. "So his emotions have changed that far!"

"But what does he want?" she asked again.

"I don't think he knows the answer himself. It's Hauser's memory working sporadically. Hillel promised to return with us tomorrow. When we discussed his case, he was as clear-minded and constructive as ever. We have methods of breaking down the foreign RNA. But I would like to know when Hauser's memory is taking over. What triggers it? How much of Hillel's former personality is left when he believes he's Hauser? None, I suppose, when he resented you for being Jewish. The pattern of his strength fluctuates, and I'm trying to devise a method of tracing it. If I could predict his next move I could control even this case, which is aggravated because Hauser was a manic-depressive. Deep depressions are difficult to cope with. They produce suicidal tendencies. Hillel has always been well balanced, and he wouldn't know how to cope with them for any length of time. A manic-depressive often gets used to his depressions and learns how to handle them. I wonder how they affect Hillel? Did he talk to you about this?"

He became aware that Karen was watching him with horror.

"You're intrigued only by the success and the challenge of this experiment," she cried bitterly. "Hillel doesn't matter to you at all. Nor do I. All you care about are your observations and deductions. I wonder if you really want to stop the experiment. Wouldn't it be much more interesting to you if it continued, with Hillel as a test animal which can talk intelligently and answer questions, might even give you the answers? This is the perfect case for you; why not prolong it? Maybe sacrifice the guinea pig at the end and look for the physiological changes in the brain? The frontal lobes might have developed or atrophied. Wouldn't that be a scientific triumph—to find out what changes RNA produces? You're not human."

Cory listened quietly, knowing that she was right. His compassion had become a thin varnish over his curiosity. He had always liked experiments that were not defined, that gave him an opportunity to travel a thousand different roads—especially when one of those roads could lead to some revolutionary result.

Suddenly all the tension, the danger, the excitement— yes, the excitement!—exploded in him. "You're not talking about me but about the nature of my profession," he said. "One thing research cannot tolerate is compromise."

"It destroys the humanity in you, if you ever had any. Was it worth it?"

"I don't know anything else," he answered.

"You're hiding behind your test tubes. You're afraid of facing yourself. Why are you so afraid of emotions?"

He looked at her quietly, hating to talk about himself. "Am I?"

"Yes! Something basic is wrong with you," Karen said bitterly.

"Who can decide what's right and what's wrong? My business is to conceive new ways of investigation and to get results backed up by proof from tests."

"What's your reward?" she demanded. "You don't work for money, so what's your compensation? Fame? Pride? There by the grace of God goes Patrick Cory, Nobel prizewinner?"

"My reward?" Cory said. "It's the moment when an idea I have conceived can be put into practice, when I know it will work. That's my reward. I don't know of any other. I certainly don't care about acknowledgment from others. It's enough for me that I know. I don't even care if others comprehend."

"I'm sorry for you," Karen said. "You're very lonely."

"I never was. Never for a moment." Cory left the room, closing the door firmly. He was sorry he upset Karen. But she was unable to realize the magnitude of this experiment, and as a woman was bound to be selfish about her private world.

He entered Hillel's room without knocking. Hillel was asleep, his face twitching in a dream, his breathing labored. Was it Hauser or Hillel who was dreaming? Would an encephalogram give the answer?

Cory sat down close to Hillel's bed and tried to understand the words he was muttering.

"Hauser," Cory said in a low voice, "Karl Hellmuth Hauser, can you hear me?" He was talking as if to a man under hypnosis.

Hillel went on moving his lips. "I know where to find him," he said, scarcely audible.

"Find whom?"

Hillel turned and pulled his legs up, like an embryo in its mother's womb.

"Find whom?" Cory asked again. He thought he had found the method he was looking for. Would a sleep induced by hypnosis be more effective? It had to be tried.

Cory touched Hillel's shoulder softly, and at once the young man opened his eyes and sat up with a start.

"I had a nightmare," he said. "Thanks for waking me up."

"What did you dream about?"

They looked into each other's eyes. A spark of suspicion and resentment flashed across Hillel's face, but as quickly as it appeared it vanished, and Hillel was talking normally.

"I don't want to have my dreams analyzed," Hillel said, and swung his legs out of bed. "It only confuses me. It has no practical use. And I don't want to be questioned now. I'm tired of it. You know I'm going to work with you, but give me a rest now. I could use it, believe me, after all we went through."

He got up and put his wallet and passport into his pocket.

"Where are you going at this hour?" Cory asked.

"You're worse than the police. I'm tired of being followed and chased by you and Karen and the Czechs, the Russians, the CIA, the East Germans. I told Slaughter to stop bothering me. I won't run away. A man has to be alone from time to time."

He walked to the door.

"Don't leave the hotel," Cory said. "We're flying out later this morning. You can't go walking about in a strange city, something might happen to you. Just think what happened to Hauser."

"This is Switzerland, the land of peace," Hillel said, and laughed. "Don't worry. Nobody's shooting anybody in Switzerland. Not even the Russians would dare."

"I'm coming with you," Cory said.

"Be my guest," Hillel answered. "I just want to get out of this room. I need fresh air. Hotel rooms give me the creeps. Let's go, Dottore."

As Cory got to the door, Hillel suddenly hit him with a vicious blow in the solar plexus, and Cory collapsed into unconsciousness.

25

It rained slowly and incessantly; gray clouds rose from the valley surrounding the town of Lugano and released their moisture in a continuing cycle.

Andres Guzman drove his big Mercedes along Lake of Lugano, past the white villas of Paradiso, over the bridge into Agno, then up the tortuous road to Vernate, where he lived. The car's wheels slid precariously on the slippery road, but Guzman was used to it. He could drive home in a dense fog without missing a turn in the road.

He was returning from Campione, the gambling casino, a no-man's-land between Switzerland and Italy. He had been lucky, and the few thousand francs he had won put him in good spirits. Not that he needed the money. Millions of francs were stashed away in his accounts at Swiss banks. When he applied for residence and the banks gave the federal government in Bern an account of his holdings, they were described as "in excess of ten million francs"—the precise sum was not mentioned, of course.

Guzman had built a house above the tiny village of Vernate; since the time of the Roman Empire the Swiss canton of Ticino had been a favorite retreat.

Guzman was content. The suit made of Harris tweed, well cut by an Italian tailor, encased his body snugly. He was a man of medium height, neck heavy and muscular like a wrestler's, barrel-cheated, stomach round like an enormous cannonball, thighs like stone columns supporting the heavy body. His short hair was bristly and gray, and he wore blue sunglasses. They gave him an air of mystery. He took them off only at night in his bedroom.

Guzman lived alone. To be alone was security. He had learned not to trust anybody, not even his closest friends. He had known times when friendship had to be ransomed for survival, and such times might come again.

The Mercedes passed Vernate, whose cobblestoned streets were barely wide enough for the car. The century-old houses were built of rocks haphazardly heaped on each other and fused with the mountainside. The farmers who lived in them grew grapes on the slopes and tended small gardens, raised chickens and goats. Except for an old couple who came in to clean and cook and whose dialect he did not understand, Guzman lived alone. When he passed the church an old woman called out to him excitedly. He drove on.

There was his house, built by a famous Swiss architect, fifty steps below the road. He parked the car in a garage by the road. As he walked down the rain-washed steps, Guzman looked at the cottony clouds that obscured the view and felt like a god drifting through the void before creation.

No sound but the rain. Guzman loved quietude. There had been too much noise in his life, guns firing, bombs dropping, planes roaring, barked commands, agonized screams that still echoed in his ears.

Though his old Cuban passport had not been renewed by Castro, the government in Bern had issued him identifications papers, certifying he was a diplomat and political refugee. He always had ample cash on hand to help the men who visited him secretly and at night. Thin-faced men, former SS, who were eternally on the run. He shipped them to Egypt or South America. But he himself stayed close to the country that he knew would call for him again. Sometimes he drove to the border, just to look at the Fatherland. Wasn't there a new party already formed, which disclaimed the guilt of starting World War II and which rightly denied any war crimes? Didn't it already have seats in the German Bundestag? It would grow in the true German spirit, and he, Guzman, who had always been close to the people, a hero, a shining example of Nordic manhood, of Teutonic courage and loyalty, who had proudly worn the skull and crossbones on his soldier's cap—he would come to power again.

Guzman shook the rain from his hat and coat and unlocked the door to his house. A couple of steps led down to a sunken living room whose huge glass windows faced the snowy mountains behind which lay Germany.

Heavy carpets noiselessly swallowed his steps. The walls were paneled in tropical wood and covered with paintings. Not the sick modern art, but solid pictures faithfully depicting the beauty of Germany, Rothenburg ob der Tauber, Nuremberg before it was leveled by bombers, Ulm, Munich, and quaint villages that still contained the best of Germany's blood. If he could not enter Germany, at least he could bring the Fatherland into his house.

He pressed a button which slid aside the big mirror concealing the bar. As the glass moved, he saw the man standing behind him.

"Hello Gesler," the man said.

Guzman immediately realized that this man was not one of his former comrades. He looked Mediterranean, Jewish, or Cuban.

"What are you doing here?" he said.

Only then did he realize that the man had called him by his real name, a name that had been buried since the day he had crawled away from the Führer's bunker over the rubble of Berlin.

Hillel's dark eyes did not leave Gesler's face. "I've wanted to visit you for years, Gesler," he said.

Gesler did not show fear; he had faced danger too often to be surprised by it. The chance that somebody would recognize him despite his blue glasses, gray hair, and stout body was always present. But this man was too young ever to have met him as Gesler.

"I don't know you," Gesler said. "And my name is Guzman, not Gesler."

He inched to the wall. In the upper drawer of the teakwood cabinet was a loaded gun.

"I think you do," Hillel said. "The last time we met was in Prague, in 1944. You questioned me about my participation in the anti-Hitler plot. Our friend Van Kungen denounced me. And since I didn't confess, because I wasn't involved, you called in a man named Metzner. He came in with four more of your killers. They held me down and Metzner castrated me with a pocketknife while you looked on. Metzner complained that he was not at his best. 'My hands are too heavy today,' he said. I was still conscious enough to hear him say it when they dragged me out of the room—number 331, the Ambassador Hotel."

"What a crazy story," Gesler said. It was curious how vividly he remembered the look on Hauser's face. "Why come here and tell me this nonsense?"

"I am Hauser."

A madman! Gesler had dealt with his kind before. He remembered one who had screamed at him as he stood at the *Leichengraben,* before he was shot and his body toppled into the trench.

"You and your kind will be the wandering Jews of the future. You will never find peace, not you, nor your children or your children's children. You will carry the mark of Cain forever!"

Gesler had been unable to get the picture of that man's face out of his mind—and now he was seeing it again. But they could not be the same. Decades had passed since then.

Gesler had reached the cabinet and pulled open the drawer.

"Don't bother," Hillel said. "I've got it."

He picked up the gun, which he had hidden in the seat of a deep easy chair.

"What do you want?" Gesler said. He knew that he was safe as long as he kept on talking.

"You must've had a lot of excitement in your life, Gesler," Hillel said, "committing crimes in the name of your Fatherland, legitimate crimes, murder and torture by law. You ruled over a concentration camp. You had people shot, hanged, beheaded, tortured, mutilated to preserve your way of life. I've had a long time to think of you. Thank God, I finally found you."

Gesler took off his glasses. The watery blue of his irises melted into the white of his eyeballs. They were small, cruel, and ugly eyes. "I don't know who fed you these stories about a man called Gesler," he said, moving closer to a small table on which stood a large heavy bronze lion. "My name is Andres Guzman. I come from Cuba. My parents were German emigrants, that's why I speak German. I have built this house with the permission of the Swiss government. You are looking at the wrong man."

"You wore a robe, striped in blue and white, when you questioned me in your room. You wore those glasses too.

"I never owned a dressing gown. I don't use them," Gesler said. "Look in my bedroom and see if I have one." He reached the table and rested his hands near the bronze lion.

"For years I knew where to find you," Hillel went on. "A few people knew about you. One of the German scientists in Baikonur told me where you lived. You ran Batista's police, then you became his ambassador to Peru. You have access to money the Nazis have hidden in Swiss banks. You're building a new cadre of murderers around you, and you're waiting for the time when you can use them." He lifted the gun. "Ten thousand nights and days I thought of you. Instead of praying I thought of you. Ten thousand times I pictured in my mind the moment I would see you again, and do to you what you've done to tens of thousands of innocent people."

"Don't be ridiculous," Gesler said.. "I don't think you're even ten thousand days old. You've never met me. Nor have I ever seen you."

Hillel looked at the steel-blue gun in his hand.

"This is what I have to do," he said. "I can't go on living without fulfilling what I'm forced to do."

"Come to your senses, man. Who told you to kill me? You seem to believe that you're a man called Hauser. Are you mutilated, as you said Hauser was? Are you? Or do you have a wife or a girl to sleep with? What is your name? Tell me! Who are you?"

Surreptitiously he grasped the bronze lion. If only he could keep this crazed man listening and talking ...

"Who are you?" he shouted in the commanding voice that had cowed so many people. At once he sensed the question disturbed the intruder. "You don't look to me like a man who can kill. It needs a special breed to murder in cold blood. You're not the type. You couldn't pull that trigger even if you wanted to. And you still haven't told me who you are."

Gesler's voice reverberated in Hillel's ears. Who was he? He was not Hauser. He was Hillel Mondoro. Hauser's depression, which he feared more than physical pain, enwrapped him, constricted his chest, inhibited his breathing. His vision narrowed to a point where he could see only Gesler's obscene mouth shouting words that hammered into his consciousness. Hillel could no longer endure the fathomless unhappiness of Hauser's mind.

Hauser must die.

Gesler hurled the bronze lion as Hillel pulled the trigger. Gesler's face exploded in crimson fragments. But Hillel did not turn his head. The heavy metal crashed into his forehead, and the world around him became dark and peaceful forever.

26

The sun had broken through the clouds, and the Corso leading along the Lake of Lugano was crowded with people. Cory walked along, watching gulls screech toward the water to gobble up crumbs thrown by the tourists.

Cory felt drained of resources. He had just left Karen at the hotel, where she had told him she believed she was pregnant. Though Cory used this news to bolster her spirits, his own mind was awhirl with new possibilities: Does foreign RNA affect the chromosomes of the genetic code? Since DNA and RNA are building blocks, would the child inherit traits of Hauser's character?

Apparently the Pandora's box he had opened was bottomless.

For Wendtland and Slaughter the Hauser case was closed and Cory knew that they were content with the outcome. They had tried to cope with an idea too abstract for them and felt their disbelief vindicated when the fantastic scheme failed. Wendtland had already left. Slaughter stayed behind at the request of the Swiss police.

The police had questioned Karen, who told them she knew nothing. She had no idea what prompted Hillel to break into a house in Vernate. He had never been to Vernate before. She had never heard of a man named Guzman, and she did not know why Hillel shot him. Cory knew that the police did not believe her.

As he walked along, trying to keep his mind free of disturbing thoughts, he saw a man standing at the rail that divided the sidewalk from the water. He recognized the unruly shock of hair, the giant body.

"What are you doing in Lugano?"

"Waiting for you." Vassilov's smile rearranged the deep lines of his face. "Your experiment was a failure, Dr. Cory."

"Not altogether," Cory answered. "We learn from negative results as much as from success. Knowing what not to do points out the right way."

"You know the right way?"

"Partly. Memory transfer can be achieved, but we also transplant character traits, inhibitions, frustrations, and hatreds. Mondoro couldn't cope with the depressions that had entered his body artificially."

"I'm convinced that Mondoro was the wrong host for Hauser's RNA. You or I, or anybody more stable, would have acted differently. I'm sure I'd have been able to record Hauser's memory unbiasedly."

"I don't think so. We all would have been forced to do what Hauser had in mind. He never wanted to give his secret away, neither to Russia nor to us. He used us to get away from you. He had other plans."

"What plans?"

"He wanted to turn back the clock. He started with Van Kungen. Only then he became aware that times had changed, though they had stood still in his memory. His dream to return to his wife didn't work out. His son, he found out, hated him. During his forced exile in Baikonur his love for his native country must have taken on monstrous proportions. Germany, purified of Nazism, would be ready to accept him, a hero wrongly accused and wrongly convicted, a hero who would turn over to his homeland one of the most valuable discoveries of the atom age: the formula for harnessing hydrogen fission for peaceful use. But Germany disillusioned him, as his wife and son did, by circumstances and by necessity."

"Is that conjecture? Though Hauser burned his notes, his memory must still have contained the formula."

"It did."

"Then Mondoro knew it all the time!" Vassilov exclaimed. "I

suspected as much. And now you know it, Cory!"

"I don't. I stopped Mondoro from telling me."

"But why?"

"Self-protection, I guess. You would never have permitted us to leave."

Vassilov shrugged.

For a moment Cory said nothing; then his face brightened. His mind was alight with the problems before it.

"We must devise a different approach to future memory transfer," he said. "First we must explore the working of enzymes, since enzymes control emotions. By purifying the RNA and using only selective molecular structures, we should come closer to creating pure memory transfer without the impurity of personal traits."

"You're a man obsessed," Vassilov said, admiringly. "You will never admit that any problem is insoluble."

"Solving problems has nothing to do with our individual desires. Science is driven by a self-propelling logic and operates quite independently of human choice and direction. It tends irresistibly toward completeness. It advances, eliminating every lesser force. Nothing can stop it."

They looked at the towering Alps, which had been hidden by gray curtains of rain. The rain had ceased, and now the peaks in the far distance stood out sharply against the translucent sky.

"It's turning into a clear day after all," Vassilov said.

"Isn't that what we're seeking in science?" Cory replied, gazing at the chain of the Ticino Alps, the Madone di Giovo, the Laghetti, the Rosso di Ribbia, the multitude of peaks covered with eternal snow, suddenly revealed before them. "For the rare day when the haze lifts, for the moment of clarity?"

fin

www.ingramcontent.com/pod-product-compliance
Lightning Source LLC
Chambersburg PA
CBHW030515020726
47494CB00004B/1106